Owen

 FARRADAY COUNTRY 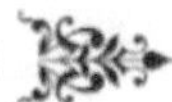 BOOK FIFTEEN

CHRIS KENISTON

Indie House Publishing

MORE BOOKS
By Chris Keniston

The Billionaire Barons of Texas
Just One Date
Just One Spark
Just One Dance
Just One Take
Just One Taste
Just One Shot
Just One Chance

Hart Land
Heather
Lily
Violet
Iris
Hyacinth
Rose
Calytrix
Zinnia
Poppy
Picture Perfect

Farraday Country
Adam
Brooks
Connor
Declan
Ethan
Finn
Grace
Hannah
Ian
Jamison

Keeping Eileen
Loving Chloe
Morgan
Neil
Owen

Honeymoon Series
Honeymoon for One
Honeymoon for Three
Honeymoon for Four
Honeymoon for Five

Aloha Romance Series:
Aloha Texas
Almost Paradise
Mai Tai Marriage
Dive Into You
Look of Love
Love by Design
Love Walks In
Shell Game
Flirting with Paradise

Surf's Up Flirts:
(Aloha Series Companions)
Shall We Dance
Love on Tap
Head Over Heels
Perfect Match
Just One Kiss
It Had to Be You
Cat's Meow

CHAPTER ONE

Some days Owen Michael Farraday wished that he could simply tap his shirt and tell Scotty to beam him up. Of course that meant that the family ranch in Oklahoma would have to be the mothership. Ideally, the beam me up concept would work more like that TV witch who twitched her nose and instantly was somewhere else. Then commuting between two states wouldn't be such a drain.

The long hot shower had been a small slice of heaven. After the almost seven-hour drive to the family home in Oklahoma, his back had let him know that despite the comfort of his nice new pickup, driving back and forth between Oklahoma and Texas was getting beyond old. The modern world had advanced to talk to computers with no need of a keyboard, communicate anywhere in the world instantly via cell phones, or if they preferred, see the smiling faces with video calls, and a slew of other sci-fi realities. How hard could inventing speed travel be? Except, if he were honest with himself, living and working in Texas and leaving the Oklahoma projects for someone else to manage held growing appeal over driving back and forth and trying to keep his mother happy while he was at it.

In the meantime, at least thanks to all the wonderful advances of modern technology, he'd been able to knock out several phone calls to unruffle some feathers on two of the Oklahoma renovations underway. Though he preferred handling business from an ergonomically comfortable chair—yeah, somewhere he'd become that old – progress while driving was still progress. The Farraday Brothers Construction crews were some of the best, able to accomplish the world without him or his brothers having to micromanage them. If only he could say the same thing about some of their subcontractors.

One in particular had been at the root of both of those phone calls. One of the interior designers they used had a nasty habit of going over budget on her work. The woman had no sense of numbers at all, but she had to have lost her mind on the Chez Gerard renovations. One of the most exclusive velvet rope restaurants in the entire state of Oklahoma, Farraday Construction had managed to beat out five of their best competition for the project. The numbers had been tight and unlike most of the projects, the contingency budget was next to nothing. His brother Neil had insisted Constance Swenson was the right choice. Considering how many times Owen had had to do battle with her over numbers, he was less than convinced the fit was right. After multiple calls with their bookkeeper, the furniture gallery, and the logistics company responsible for the delivery of the imported chairs—from France, no less— he wouldn't mind wringing her pretty little neck. Except that was one thing his mother and Aunt Eileen would agree on—they'd both kill him.

Now it was up to him and his brothers to find a way to offset the unexpected expense of imported restaurant chairs. Towel drying his hair, he shook his head wondering, what was wrong with Made in the U.S.A.?

The sound of booted heels stomping up the wooden steps of the old ranch house resonated down the hall. He'd always thought his family home was a comfortable place, but it didn't hold a candle to his Uncle Sean's spread.

"About time you got here." His identical twin brother Paxton's voice boomed from down the hall. "We don't have all day."

As his brother crossed his room in a few long strides, the same towel now wrapped around Owen's hips, he flung open the bathroom door. "For what?"

"Tomorrow's design meeting on the new ghost hotel has been pushed up to today."

"We really have to find a new name for the place. You

can't keep calling this segment we're filming of the ghost town renovation, Ghost Hotel."

"Don't see why not." Pax shrugged. "Anyhow, Neil is still in Tuckers Bluff, so you're going to have to meet with Harriet. Fortunately, this is only the prelim gathering. Going over the plans Neil drew up and the budget you've laid out as well as sharing a few photos of the *not* ghost hotel, and discussion of the direction we're going in."

Thank heaven Neil hadn't insisted on that woman who had given him a headache the size of Texas. "Why me?"

"I told you. Neil is still in Texas and you're here."

"So are you." Why his brother wanted him to meet with the design team was beyond him. He was just a numbers man. "You're a landscape designer and she's an interior designer. The two of you probably speak the same language."

"Plants and wallpaper are unrelated."

"You're both creative. I'm all about numbers and spreadsheets. You speak her language."

"If I didn't have to pick up the order for the downtown project I would, but last time the nursery stuck us with too many substandard plants. If they botch this, they're done. Even if it means driving to the next county for a decent nursery, but I don't have time to drive back and forth if they try it again today, so I have to go with the crew for pick up. Show the nursery who they're dealing with."

All right, he'd give his brother a pass. This wouldn't be the first or last time a vendor put their best foot forward until they thought the Farradays were no longer checking. Still. "Why the rush? Why not tomorrow as scheduled?"

Paxton shrugged a shoulder and flashing a lopsided smirk intended to be a smile, Owen knew before his twin opened his mouth that he was not going to like what Pax said. "Something about a standing appointment for a mani-pedi and not wanting to lose her slot."

Had his brother really just said that to him? Paxton wanted Owen to piss off his mother and do Neil's job because the lady wanted her toes polished?

"Don't look at me that way." Paxton held his hand up.

"I don't argue with a woman and her beauty routine."

"Harriet is as old as Mom. What beauty routine?"

"Ours is not to reason why…"

Lord love a duck. He hated it when his brother quoted Tennyson. Inevitably it always meant he was about to get suckered into something he didn't want to do—like today. "Ours is just to do or die." If you can't beat them join them.

"If it makes you feel any better, Tammy doesn't have the time to commute to Texas, but she is going to be in on the meeting."

That brought a smile to his face. He and Tammy had been friends for so long he'd lost track and with this renovation of the old ghost town for the Construction Cousins Reality TV series he and his brothers had committed to, he hadn't seen her in a month of Sundays. They'd tried dating a time or two, but always came to the same conclusion; they made better friends than sweethearts. "It'll be good to see her."

"So you're going?" A sincere grin pulled at his brother's lips.

"You know I will, but you also do realize Mom is in the kitchen cooking up every favorite food I ever mentioned liking. She expects me to spend the rest of the afternoon with her. If I leave now she's going to be beyond pissed. I don't even want to think about her reaction when she finds out that I'm only staying in Oklahoma a few days. I have to be back in Tuckers Bluff on Monday to go over changes with the film crew and then I have to finalize the details with Neil for the Ghost Town Palooza. You know how fired up Mom is over all the time we're spending away from home. Since learning we're hanging out in Tuckers Bluff she's almost impossible." He hadn't told any of his brothers how often his mother had been texting him with excuses why he needed to come home quickly. He had no idea why she had picked him as the brother to approach, but as far as he knew, she wasn't saying much of anything to the others.

Wrapping his hand around his neck, Pax shook his head and sank onto the corner of the bed. "I swear, something about Texas brings out the worst in our mother. She spent twenty minutes carrying on about Neil and Morgan abandoning her and I won't repeat the things she said about Tuckers Bluff."

"Nothing we haven't heard a thousand times before." Though he really did wish someone had a clue why their mother resented Texas and the other branches of the Farradays more than income taxes.

Pax pushed to his feet. "Now that we've settled that. You're meeting with Harriet and I'm off to the nursery."

"Not so fast." He grabbed a shirt out of the closet. "I may be stepping in for Neil, but you're telling Mom I have to leave."

"Crud." Pax sighed. "Fine. But you'll owe me."

Owen merely rolled his eyes and tossed the towel into the hamper. What else could possibly go wrong today?

"Oh man, that's a beauty." Standing in her friend and coworker Tammy' office, Connie admired the barley twist mahogany table that Tammy had found at an estate sale. Every so often they'd stumble onto the perfect item at the most unexpected places. "I absolutely love it when we find a bargain that's just spot-on. That horrible silver candelabra that Mrs. Benson is so fond of will look great on that table."

"Thank heavens. I freely admit I was struggling with how to display that gaudy piece without making the whole room look like a bad set design for a horror movie. But mostly I'm just happy this will help balance out the overages. The budget allowed a thousand dollars for this piece. Now I can shift the unused eight hundred to offset the cost of the chandelier." Tammy spun about and pulled out a silver shopping bag. "Since I didn't have to spend all afternoon scouring the city for that piece, I stopped a few minutes at the new boutique on Fillmore Street."

Connie had been so wrapped up trying to give that arrogant French chef everything he wanted, rob Peter to pay Paul, and convince everyone that she had all the spending for Gerard's fancy restaurant under control, that she'd not had a single moment to go check out the newest shop on what was slowly becoming the hot artsy area of town.

"What do you think?" Tammy held what would no doubt be a short, snug fitting dress in the most gorgeous shade of azure blue.

"Oh my." She reached out to finger the delicate beading.

Tammy frowned. "Is that good or bad?"

"Good. With your figure, that dress will look gorgeous on you."

Her coworker's face lit up with delight. "Thanks!"

"As a matter of fact, I just might borrow this little number from you one of these days." There were benefits to having good friends the same size as you. From time to time she and her friends had been known to lend out formal dresses through the years. A gesture her budget greatly appreciated.

Holding the dress against her, Tammy twirled in place. "Now all I need is someplace to wear it."

"I hear Owen Farraday is in town again. I doubt it would take much persuasion to get him to take you someplace worthy of that dress."

Tammy's forehead crinkled before she sighed. "I suppose, but it would be a shame to waste this dress on just a friend. This puppy deserves an honest to God date with a guy who will kiss you goodnight and curl your toes."

"You're telling me Owen's a lousy kisser?" Connie found that hard to believe. All those Farradays were chips off the same block and many a woman would kill to get them alone. Then again, being good looking was no guarantee of anything else.

"I didn't say that, but for me there's no spark, no magic. It's almost like kissing a brother."

"Ick." Connie hadn't meant to say that out loud, but the words just gave her the chills and not in a nice way. Though, she'd always thought that Tammy still liked Owen more than she'd let on and that it was Mr. Penny Pincher who had ended their brief romantic liaisons. Another reason not to be thrilled with Mr. Owen Farraday.

Tammy chuckled and shook her head, more proof that she still carried a torch for the guy. Twirling one more time, Tammy slipped the dress back neatly into the bag. "Some day. What time do you have to be back at the restaurant?"

"I don't." The last minute reprieve from yet another meeting with the restaurant people and probably the Farraday bookkeeper was a true blessing. Chez Gerard had proven to be one of the most challenging jobs she'd done in a very long time. Not that this project was any different than any other commercial endeavor, it was just that she was learning the hard way that the French had a different perspective on life. Sometimes it was kind of fun, but others, like the fiasco over the chairs, not so much. "Apparently there's a bug going around and he's down to half the kitchen staff, so they have twice as much work to do and Gerard does not want anyone who doesn't cook taking up space."

"Taking up space?" Tammy chuckled. "Nice of him."

"Well, he might have said it a little differently, but I got the message nonetheless."

"I have to admit, I don't think I care for that man very much." Tammy shrugged. "But then again, it's no secret that they don't care much for us. So I guess that makes us even."

Connie chuckled. "That's one way to look at it."

"Darn it." Now on all fours, Tammy was in front of a cabinet in her office, pulling the contents out from the shelves and placing them on the floor beside her. "I know I shoved those swatches in here somewhere. They're in a plastic bag from the Design Loft."

"Let me help." Even though the cabinet Tammy was searching through was in her office, it was shared by all the staff for storing product samples and project leftovers.

The problem, of course, was that with each project that ended, the stash of goodies in the wall of lower cabinets was replicating at an alarming pace.

Tammy pushed to her feet. "You'd think Harriet could afford to use pull out shelves. I'm getting too old to be on my knees searching for a needle in a haystack."

If Tammy, five years Connie's junior, was too old, then Connie was S.O.L. "Just where is Harriet?"

"She ran out to grab a burger. Should be back any minute." On her feet and dusting off her hands, Tammy sighed. "Maybe they're in the break room."

"Good idea." Still on all fours, having moved to the next cabinet, Connie waved at her friend. "Search in there and I'll keep digging here."

"Sounds like a plan. Thanks."

Her head buried deep in the lower cabinets, tossing out paint chips, grout samples, wood flooring samples, vinyl floor strips, Connie was convinced any second now she would come across a kitchen sink.

"Well, hey there gorgeous."

The deep male voice was unexpected. She'd barely managed to ease herself a few inches out of from the cabinet when a very large hand landed smack on her derriere, snapping her upright and smacking her head hard against the top of the cabinet. *What the hell?*

CHAPTER TWO

Oh, blast. The last thing Owen had meant to do was startle Tammy into bumping her head. He really should have thought that coming up behind her and patting her rump might be a bit too startling. After all, that was the kind of behavior that found many a man in front of the human resource executives. But they'd teased, and wrestled, and shared a friendly pat from time to time; still, he should have known better. "I'm sorry, I didn't mean to startle you. Are you okay?"

"What did you do now, big boy?" The sound of Tammy's voice had him spinning around faster than an old fashioned top.

Sure enough, ten feet in front of him, leaning in the doorway, her arms filled with a tall pile of fabric, Tammy both shook her head and grinned at him. The real question was, if Tammy was across the room, whose well-rounded rump had he just patted? His head whipped from Tammy to the person backing out from the cabinet. A sense of sheer panic shot up his spine. What had he done? Visions of human resource interrogations and lawsuits sprang to mind.

Giggling softly, Tammy set the pile on the nearby table and shaking her head slowly from side to side, patted him on the shoulder. "No offense, but you look like you're about to heave. It's okay. Connie won't shoot you."

Connie? Again, his gaze snapped from Tammy to the woman now straightening in place. Brushing her hands together, her expression said nothing. He had no clue if she was going to laugh it off or haul off and hit him. He deserved the latter.

One eyebrow high on her forehead, Constance—

Connie—Swenson stared daggers at him. "I prefer to be greeted with a handshake."

If he could, he'd crawl under a rock. Hat in hand, he spun the rim of the old Stetson around and around between his fidgety fingers. "Please accept my apology. I thought you were Tammy. You have similar, uhm, I mean from behind, uh…" Squeezing his eyes tightly shut for a moment he wondered if there was any way to get his size twelve foot out of his mouth. "Please accept my apology."

Heaving a deep sigh, she bobbed her head. "Apology accepted."

Relieved she was neither laughing nor swinging at him, he turned to Tammy, who was still giggling under her breath. "Where's Harriet?"

"Planning on feeling her up too?" The grin on Connie's face did nothing to offset the curt tone.

"Connie!" Tammy's voice came out sharp and scolding, like a mother reproving her toddler.

"Sorry." She waved her hand at Tammy and Owen. "Now it's my turn to apologize. That was uncalled for."

"No," Owen shook his head, "I deserved that."

"Let's say we just move on." Tammy smiled. "And Harriet is held up. She wants us to go ahead and go over the plans and for Connie to sit in for her till she arrives and will catch up."

With the conference room table covered in architectural drawings, the three of them went through every inch of the initial plans.

"I have to say," Tammy removed the leather weights and folded up one of the plans, "I wish I were in on this. I think this has the potential to be one of the most interesting and fun projects we've ever been involved in. I mean, imagine bringing a ghost town back to life."

Connie had said very little during the meeting. Probably because it wasn't going to be her project, possibly because she was still sore at him. Whether because he'd scolded her over the restaurant budget, or the foolish smack to her backside when he thought he was greeting Tammy, was anyone's guess. Now she merely bobbed her head at her coworker. "Are you going to salvage the crown moldings?"

"We're certainly going to try. Whatever is damaged will be replaced with a plaster copy. We've got a guy in Dallas who does amazing work. No one will know the difference."

Again, she nodded, lips pressed tightly together, but said nothing.

"Well." Tammy straightened. "I may not have the time to do this job myself, but I may find a little time to go and peek. I bet it's going to be amazing." She spun to face Owen. "And I bet it's a blast working for a TV show."

"Oh, yeah. A blast," he muttered.

"Do I detect a problem?" Harriet came through the double doors. "Sorry I'm so late. Some days I feel like our little corner of the world is getting too darn big."

And thank heaven for that. All the growth was keeping Farraday Construction busy and in the money. Though he'd be the first one to admit watching his cousins and brothers happily playing house was enough to make him want to find a love of his own and give up the city rat race to settle down in Tuckers Bluff. That, of course, was nothing more than crazy thinking. Despite how it looked, or what the town said about the dogs, wives didn't just fall out of trees.

"I liked the cake balls better when Toni used more flavor." Seated at the Farraday kitchen table, Ruth Ann tossed a coin into the pot.

"You mean more booze." Fanning her cards out, whether Sally May was grinning at her hand or her comment on the cake balls was anyone's guess.

"Tomayto, Tomahto." Ruth Ann shrugged off the comment.

"I'll take two." Eileen stared at her hand. So far she'd been dealt few winning hands. More than once she'd gotten up to refresh the cake balls or drinks, but really, she'd done so more often than necessary in hopes of changing up her game. So far no such luck. "Besides, I think after that first taste testing before Adam and Meg's wedding, Toni is a bit skittish on adding too much liquor to those balls."

"Too bad." Nora folded her cards in her hand and let out a deep sigh. "I love these the way they are, but they did have just a little bit of kick before."

"I'm simply going to have to get Toni to make me some samples so I can do a before and after test." Morgan's wife Valerie had been roped into the poker game a few months back and now every chance that time permitted, she joined in on the game. With the next stage of the ghost town project not picking up till Monday when Paxton and Owen returned from Oklahoma, and Neil and Morgan returned from a project in Austin, poker was moved to the ranch for an all day marathon.

"There's an idea. Sort of like movies." Sally May waved her arm at her friend. "Folks who saw an original movie tend to like it better than the remake, and folks who saw the remake first tend to like it better than the original. We'll see if the same applies to cake balls."

"Deal." Valerie drew her three cards and smiled. The woman might enjoy sitting in on a game from time to time, but bless her heart, a poker face she would never have.

"Oh, which reminds me." Eileen waved at the stack of albums on the buffet in the dining room. "I pulled out the old photos of the kids growing up that I promised to find for you. The two on top have a bunch of your husband and his brothers when they'd visit the ranch."

"Oh, really!" Valerie eyed the other room and Eileen could tell she was itching to take a peek. It took all of five minutes for the round to come to an end and Valerie to take the pot with her full house before she pushed to her feet. "Go ahead and deal me out this round. I want to take a quick look."

"Actually." Ruth Ann stood and stretched her back. "I say we take a break to make lunch and then pick up the next game."

"I'm in for that." Sally May stood and bent left then right. "Besides, I wouldn't mind looking at some of those photo myself. Seems like just yesterday and eons ago at the same time."

As Eileen and the others put together her version of a Reuben sandwich with leftover corned beef, Valerie and Nora moved the albums to the dining room table.

"Good grief," Nora flipped the pages of one album, "how can you tell who is who? All these boys look alike!"

Handing her a plate with a sandwich and sweet potato chips, Eileen looked over her shoulder. "This one on the left is Adam. Next to him is Ian. Beside him is Morgan."

A sweet smile took over Valerie's lips as she ran her finger across the old photograph. "Look at that hat. Isn't he adorable?"

"Looks to be about ten years old or so." Eileen couldn't help grinning herself. At times raising six boys was a handful, but her heart was always full of love and happy memories.

"Wow. This is an old sucker." Ruth Ann took a bite of her sandwich, took another second to moan her delight with Eileen's secret sauce recipe, and then pointed to the open page of one of the larger scrapbook album. "Is this Sean?"

Eileen shifted around the table to see. "Yep. He must have been about twenty then. I forgot we even had this old album. It's one of a few his mother kept." She flipped the page. "Here they are all together. Sean and his cousins Patrick and Brian."

"Dang. Those Farraday genes are strong. Makes you wonder what happened to the mom's genes." Nora chuckled softly.

"Oh. Here's Brian and Anne. They look so young," Sally May said.

Shifting closer, Eileen squinted. "That's not Brian." She pulled the album out of her friend's hand and held it up close. "That's Patrick."

"Really?" Dorothy, another of the long time members of the Ladies Afternoon Social Club, and Becky's grandmother, leaned in closer. "They look awfully close for brother and sister-in -law."

It took Eileen a few minutes of staring at the photo for all the details to come together. "I seem to remember Helen mentioning once in passing that Patrick and Anne dated briefly. Then Brian came home from college and the rest is history."

"Really?" Valerie slowly flipped through the next page or so. "So what you're telling me is that two brothers had the same taste in women?"

She supposed that was one way to put it. Though staring at the pictures in front of her, Eileen had to admit, the Oklahoma cousins' dad Patrick and the Austin cousins' mom Anne, looked awfully cozy. Another page flipped and something caught her eye. Patrick stood grinning happily with Anne tucked into the crook of his shoulder. Sporting a matching grin, Anne's left hand splayed open across his chest. Flipping back a page or two, Eileen took note of Anne's ringless fingers. Turning back to the photo of the grinning couple, Anne's left hand clearly had a new ring. *Holy moly.* Was that an engagement ring?

As much as Connie hated to admit it, concentrating on anything to do with the hotel remodel was nearly impossible. Thankfully, this wasn't her project so paying attention wasn't a priority. What she couldn't decide was what had her more discombobulated: the feel of the large, warm hand on her backside for barely an instant, or why she couldn't stop thinking about it.

This wasn't the first or last time she'd spent time with Owen Farraday. Granted, every last Farraday was a chip off the old handsome and charming block, but she'd never given any of them a second thought outside of their professional relationship. As a matter of fact, Owen was a bit bossy and single minded. She'd much rather deal with Paxton or Morgan any day of the week. Which begged the new question, why wasn't she mad as a hornet? I mean, in today's society that was no way to greet a business associate. Unless…unless she was right about Tammy's feelings for him and these two were more than just good friends.

And if there was? What did it matter? She did not have any interest in Owen Farraday. The man was both stubborn and unreasonable. He'd never given her a chance to explain about the chairs. She still wasn't sure if he knew that she hadn't broken the budget—or as he had put it—smashed the budget. Even though Tammy was right and the ghost town venture looked and sounded like the meaty type of project any designer would love to sink her teeth into, the last thing she wanted was to work another deal with Owen Farraday.

She'd been sitting at her desk, staring at the same four lines on her computer screen since Harriet had finally arrived for the meeting and Connie had excused herself. No matter how many times she scanned the screen, she just couldn't focus. After debating with herself all that time, she decided she really needed to get out more. Date a little. No person should be this distracted by a mere pat on the butt. At least no person with a decent social life. She was going to have to get one. A social life that is.

"I really do wish I had time for this project." Tammy crossed the threshold to her office and sank into the chair beside her desk.

"Not me." She hoped that sounded more convincing to Tammy than it did to Connie's ears.

"Have you lost your mind? What could be more fun than bringing a rundown old building back to life?"

"Winning the lottery?" Dumb answer but sometimes a little humor went a long way when something was bothering her.

Tammy shrugged. "I know you're kidding, but I have to agree that would be nice. But I'd still want to refurbish that old hotel, even if I was richer than Oprah."

She couldn't blame her. The project was definitely different. And speaking of different, Owen Farraday once again popped into her thoughts. "So just how close are you and Owen?"

"Just friends." Tammy shook her head. "I'm telling you, we tried that. More than once. He really is like a brother."

"Does he always grab women he's *just friends* with?"

Tammy sighed and lifted one brow at her friend and

coworker. "He did not grab you. It was a friendly pat. And no, he doesn't always greet me like that. But had it been me, I would have laughed at his silliness and I think he knew that.

"Hm." Connie wasn't convinced. The guy was successful, good looking, bossy, and stubborn. He probably thought he could do whatever he wanted with anyone and no one would complain. The more she learned about the money man of this family, the less she liked him.

"Now Paxton?" Tammy laughed and batted her lashes. "Wouldn't mind getting to know him a little better."

Okay, so maybe Tammy really didn't have the hots for Owen, but that didn't change how Connie felt. Thank heaven this project was going to be Harriet's problem and not hers. She'd just about had enough of Owen Farraday.

CHAPTER THREE

"Yes, Mom." Owen tossed another shirt into his bag. He'd not bothered bringing a large suitcase with him, but now that it was clear his next trip back to Oklahoma was not happening anytime soon, he preferred not to do laundry so often. Since the film crew would not need to capture the remodeling of every single room, their crew was scheduled to begin working on two of the three floors of the hotel first thing Monday morning. Supervising demolition was as important as monitoring construction. The only problem was his mother didn't see things the same. "I promise, first break I get, I'll be back."

"Yeah, Mom." Paxton once again had his brother's back. The two had made a habit of taking care of each other probably since the day they were born. "No matter what, this is home."

And as usual, Paxton always had the right words to make their mother smile. A weak but sincere smile on her face, she patted her younger-by-five-minutes twin son on the cheek. "Always and forever. Though I'm still waiting for my sons to fill this big old house with grandbabies."

"Patience, woman. Patience." Owen kissed the top of his mother's head in time for her to spin around and squeeze him tightly.

"I love you boys. And don't forget it."

"Mom," Pax almost whined. "We're going to Texas, not Antarctica."

"Might as well be the moon." She took a step back and forced a smile. "I put some food together for the ride." Her grin brightened. "I baked banana bread. Your favorite. It will have to tide you over till you come back."

Looping an arm around her waist, he tugged her against him and kissed her cheek. He didn't dare tell her that when it came to his favorite baked bread, no one could hold a candle to Aunt Eileen's. "Love you, Mom."

"And I love you." She pulled away and straightened her shoulders. "Better get going. Don't want you driving those lonesome roads in the pitch of night."

"No, Ma'am."

The two brothers headed down the stairs and out the front door. Outside, their dad was climbing out of his truck. "Was afraid I'd miss you."

Owen returned the man's hug and whispered in his ear. "Not you too?"

"Me too what?"

"Never mind." Owen gave him one last hug. He really did miss his father. They'd always had a close relationship and it never occurred to Owen as he and his brothers were building their business that one day he might be spending more time away from Oklahoma and less and less time with his parents.

"Let him go, Patrick. I don't want him driving those barren roads in the dark."

"You should come visit. We'd love to show you the project."

At the same exact moment his dad muttered *maybe*, his mother barked a resounding *no*. Some things never changed.

Only an hour into the long drive home, he realized that he really didn't want to keep doing this drive. Maybe next time he'd fly. He'd also come to another realization. Oddly enough over the course of the last year, he'd come to think of Tuckers Bluff as home as much as Oklahoma. Maybe more. Of course he loved and missed his parents, but not as much as he might have thought. Another few hours and his mind drifted from the hotel project, to Tammy and what a shame they were better suited as friends, to Connie and what had possessed him to smack the woman's butt. He'd kicked all of the above around over and over and was thrilled when his phone rang. Anything to get his mind off the treadmill it had embarked on.

"How's it going?" Paxton had needed to run a couple of errands before leaving Oklahoma, but he expected to reach the ranch in time for supper.

"Long. You on the road?"

"I am. I should be arriving about an hour behind you."

"Good. I'm sure Aunt Eileen will be happy when we're off the road."

"At least someone will be happy."

"Say again."

"Just got off the phone with Morgan." Something in Pax's tone had him straightening in his seat.

"Is he all right?"

"Other than grumbling about physical therapy on his ankle, yes, he's fine."

Owen waited another moment for his brother to speak. "So what's going on?"

A deep sigh traveled through the phone. "Tammy called him. Harriet slipped going down the front steps. Broken pelvis."

"Ouch."

"That about covers it. That also means she can't do the hotel job."

If it meant working with Tammy again, he wouldn't complain. Harriet was a lovely lady, but working with his friend wouldn't be a hardship. "Tammy will do a good job for us."

"I'm sure she would. There's just one problem."

The job had barely started and already his brothers were throwing problems at him. "How much is this problem going to cost us?"

"Nothing. Yet."

"Yet?"

"Tammy isn't filling in for Harriet. Connie is."

"Some days I wonder if I should have bothered getting out

of bed." Connie closed the lid on her suitcase, hoping there was a laundromat in this Podunk town if she got stuck in Texas longer than expected. "And I still don't understand why I need to drive all the way to Tuckers Bum Texas."

"Bluff not Bum." Tammy bit back a smile.

"Whatever. The point is that the work isn't anywhere near far enough along for me to need to do my job."

"What are you grumbling about? You're going to be on national television." Tammy dropped her hands on her hips. "If you think we're busy now, once this episode airs on TV, our phones are going to be ringing off the hook."

While more business was never something to complain about, Connie wasn't all that sure she wanted that much more. Harriet was becoming more and more demanding and less and less appreciative of how much she and Tammy did for a company that wasn't theirs. Harriet had them stretched pretty thin at the moment. And why their boss thought Connie could spare time to go to West Texas at this stage of the game was beyond her. She didn't even want to contemplate what that old ghost town had in store for her. Based on the shooting schedule she saw, she could be stuck in Texas for weeks, or longer.

"You'll be staying at the B&B in Tuckers Bluff for this trip. When filming starts, you'll probably be bunking at the B&B at the ghost town."

"Marvy." She did her best not to sneer instead of smile. Not that Connie had anything against bed and breakfasts, she just preferred her own bed and to skip breakfast.

"Oh, come on. Think how much fun it's going to be working with all those Farradays."

That was exactly what she was trying not to think of. In general, the Farradays were a very nice family, she just wished that any brother besides Owen was her contact on this project. "Fun, like beauty, is in the eye of the beholder. Some people think jumping out of an airplane is fun."

Tammy sighed and shook her head. "Try to make the best of this. I promise. It's going to be fun."

"Right—fun." She put a bit more effort into smiling, waved to her friend on her way out the door, tossed her bag into the back of her small SUV, and climbed into the front seat muttering 'have fun' over and over. Maybe if she said it often enough she'd start to believe it.

The first hour and a half of the drive was spent on the phone with Harriet. It had taken that long for her boss to share every thought and idea she'd ever had for remodeling a hotel. Sometimes having Harriet micromanage every idea was exhausting. Anyone listening would think Connie had never worked a project on her own before. It would also sound like she'd never worked with a Farraday. Considering she'd done both, and already had ideas from the presentation the other day, she was more than ready to end the call. At least there was one bright side to being clear across the vast state of Texas: no Harriet looking over her shoulder.

A few more conversations with Tammy, the drapery workshop for the project that Harriet was going to take over as soon as the doctor gave her the okay, and the logistics liaison for Chez Gerard's infamous chairs and she was delighted to realize that she'd managed to kill hours of time and was leaving the barren, boring West Texas countryside and pulling into a typical one traffic light small Texas town.

Despite her frustration at the last minute change and having to drive halfway to China, she found herself smiling at the quaint little town. Her grin broadened at the huge neon sign announcing the Silver Spurs Café. She'd crossed over the border into Texas more than once hitting up the design district of Dallas, but Dallas was a far cry from West Texas and the café name beautifully hammered that reality home. A cute little boutique with a cute cursive sign announcing Sisters caught her eye. If time permitted she'd have to check it out. The Cut N Curl, and a wall of old fashioned hair dryers visible through the massive single pane window had her debating what was more small townish: the name or the hair dryers. By the time she reached the street to turn onto for the bed and breakfast, she'd noticed the pub O'Fearadaigh's and wondered why the odd choice of spelling. So close to Farraday, the name couldn't be a coincidence.

Turning the corner, she spotted the refurbished B&B. The place was even prettier in person than in the online photos. Perhaps the silver lining to this impromptu visit.

A pretty redhead came bouncing down the front steps as Connie pulled up to the curb. The woman smiled and waved cheerfully. "You must be Constance?"

Slamming the car door shut behind her, she nodded and extended her hand. "I am, but call me Connie, please."

"Connie it is. I'm Margaret Farraday, but my friends call me Meg."

Another Farraday. How had she missed that? "Nice to meet you, Meg."

"Let me help you with your luggage." The friendly innkeeper stepped in closer as Connie pulled her carryon out from the backseat.

"No need. I believe in traveling light."

This time the lady spit out a bubble of laughter. "You may be the only woman on the planet who knows how to pull that off. Follow me and we'll settle you in."

Up the steps and into the grand foyer, Connie blinked. The photos most definitely did not misrepresent. "This is lovely."

She didn't think the woman could smile any wider, but she did. "Thank you. You must be tired after the long drive."

"Just a little stiff."

"Good. Then you'll be able to join us for a cup of tea and a snack."

At the very moment the word snack escaped Meg's lips, Connie got a whiff of something absolutely heavenly. "Would that wonderful aroma have anything to do with this snack?"

Again, the woman flashed a toothy smile and bobbed her head. "It would. My sister-in-law keeps me well supplied in fresh baked goods. That wonderful scent is blueberry muffins in one oven and cranberry scones in another."

"Oh my. I have a weakness for scones."

"Don't we all." Meg opened a door at the top of the

stairs and waved Connie inside. "I hope you'll be comfortable."

Comfortable? She'd slept in five star hotels that weren't as inviting as this luscious room. "I'm sure I will be more than comfortable."

"There are hangers in the closet, towels in the bathroom, and if you need extra pillows or blankets you can ask me or help yourself to whatever you need in the hall linen closet."

"Sounds like a deal." She resisted the urge to spin in place and toss herself onto the massive four poster bed. There was little doubt in her mind that she'd most likely sink into the mattress like an angel on a cloud.

"Oh, and I almost forgot." Meg took a step in retreat toward the door. "I have strict orders from Aunt Eileen to bring you to the ranch for Sunday supper. Most of the family has been there since after church."

"That won't be necessary. I can grab a bite at the café or maybe the pub if they serve food."

"They do," Meg nodded, "but I'd rather disobey the Pope than Aunt Eileen."

Connie's concern must have shown on her face because Meg didn't wait for her to make an excuse.

"There's no hurry if you need to rest, but trust me when I tell you that you don't want to miss Aunt Eileen's lasagna. The woman may have Irish ancestors, but she cooks like an Italian kitchen goddess."

Something about the determination in Meg's gaze told Connie this was one battle she wasn't going to win.

"Oh good," a perky brunette bounded up the stairs, "you're here."

Connie looked from the woman grinning at her as if they were old friends, to her hostess, then over her shoulder to see if there was someone else nearby the brunette was talking to.

"I have to tell you," the brunette continued, "we're all very excited about bringing our little ghost town back to life, but the hotel is the one part that I have been dying to see."

Meg waved at the brunette. "Connie, this is my sister-in-law Becky. She's married to Declan the police chief."

"Nice to meet you, and whatever you're baking smells absolutely wonderful."

"Baking?" Becky laughed loudly, shaking her head. "No, ma'am. That's Toni. Brooks' wife."

"Oh." She turned to Meg. "I'm sorry. I just assumed…"

Becky waved her hand, palm out. "No need. There are a lot of us. With six brothers and two cousins from Austin, and now the construction cousins staying in town, there are a lot of Farraday sisters-in-law."

"We're just hoping," Meg chimed in, "that Uncle Patrick and Aunt Mariah will warm up to the idea of Tuckers Bluff, but that's a story for another day."

From the look on the two ladies' faces, there was definitely a story there. Apparently there was a lot to learn about this small town, *and* the Farradays. Not that any of it was her business. The sooner she got to the ghost town and took care of the preliminaries, the sooner she could get back to Oklahoma and her normal life.

CHAPTER FOUR

"Sweet." Owen's twin stared down at the latest renderings for the ghost town project. "I have to admit, I couldn't see it."

Owen bobbed his head. "I'm with you. When Neil said he could find a way to put a bathroom in every room I thought the man was crazy, but he did it. When he brought back these latest drawings adding suites, he blew me away."

"I think adding an additional floor of penthouse suites is going to be a bit pricey, but it's the best way to find a reputable company to take over management." Paxton rolled up the blueprints. "Who's going to convince the network to pay for it?"

As if his brother didn't already know who was going to be stuck with that fun job. Owen had been the money man for the family business for as long as he'd held his real estate license. At first tasked with finding the good deals and projects, quickly he became the man in charge of selling those projects as well as bringing them in on budget. Of course he would be the one tasked to convince the network sponsors on what a phenomenal business move adding another floor would be for the hotel, the town, and of course, the show.

"What has you two looking so serious?" Their Uncle Sean strolled into his office and looked over Owen's shoulder.

"Neil outdid himself." Paxton opened the massive pages out on the desk.

Squinting at the page, Sean Farraday ran his finger along the lines, then flipped the page and smiled. "Penthouse suites. Nice."

"I mentioned to Neil that we had a lot of interest in a luxury spa adjoining the hotel and the next day I had these new drawings."

"The city council approved it?"

Paxton shrugged. "Sort of."

One eyebrow shot up on Sean's forehead. "Sort of?"

"What my dear brother means is that yes they approve as long as the town isn't going to have to cover the extra cost."

"Which means the sponsors have to be convinced it's a smart move."

"It is," Uncle Sean agreed.

"I know that." Owen pointed to his twin. "And he knows that. But it's my job to convince the penny pinching sponsors of that."

"What? Are we having a party in here?" Hands on her hips, Aunt Eileen stood under the doorway. "Adam and Meg just drove up. I want the whole family together when our guest arrives."

"Guest?" Owen turned to face his aunt.

"Didn't I mention we're having company?"

Both Owen and Paxton shook their heads in perfect synchronization. The movements reminded him of how alike they used to be. As adults their personalities had taken them in two different directions, but so many of their gestures and expressions were carbon copies. It was why as kids it was too much fun confusing people. Heck, if their parents knew how often the two brothers switched places to help out with dates, tests, and just plain entertaining trickery, their parents would ground them for the rest of their lives.

Aunt Eileen shrugged. "The decorator lady is joining us for supper."

Before Owen could utter a word, the woman had turned on her heel and scurried down the hall. Wasn't it bad enough he was going to have to work bringing Connie up to speed on the project for the next few days, did it have to start with the family dinner?

After a fifteen minute power nap on the world's most comfortable bed, Connie was ready to face whatever the world threw her way. From the ride to the Farraday ranch, she'd learned that even though six Oklahoma brothers seemed like a lot to her, the Farraday clan was rather prolific. And somehow, a good chunk of the massive family would be gathering for Sunday supper.

"Welcome." A walking poster child for tall, dark, and handsome stood smiling at her from the open doorway.

"Thank you."

As she approached the door, a strong arm shot out at her. "I'm Brooks."

"The baker's husband." It wasn't really a question. But there were a lot of Texas Farradays to keep straight. At least she'd worked at some point or other with most of the Oklahoma Farradays.

"Hello." Connie could only assume the strong bubbly voice coming from the woman quickly approaching had to be the famed Aunt Eileen. "I can't tell you how happy I am to meet you. Welcome."

"Thank you. It's a pleasure to meet you too." From some of the stories she'd heard, Connie thought the family had to be exaggerating about the larger than life family matriarch, but if the stuffing squeezing hug she'd just received was any indication, this woman was indeed a force to be reckoned with.

"And this fine fellow is Gray." Eileen Farraday leaned over and scratched the ear of the dog sitting patiently at their feet.

"Here we go again." Brooks shook his head and turned into the living room, muttering something about *who let the dang dog into the house and needing a new suit.*

None of what the man said made any sense to her, but whatever his problem was, it was none of her business.

"Don't you pay any never mind to my nephew." Eileen's smile never faltered. "Come make yourself at home. Supper is almost ready to be served. You're in for a treat, Toni has been baking since she got here. No doubt we're all going to put on a few pounds."

The dog who had sat quietly beside them let out a low woof and took off down the hall, his nails clacking loudly on the wooden floor. A few steps into the room and she could see the dog once again sitting with Paxton on his knee scratching the animal's furry neck. Beside the easy going landscaper, Owen stared down at his brother, his stern expression a fraction shy of a frown. How was it the two looked so much alike and yet were so different?

At the same moment that the dog brushed up against Owen for another scratch, Paxton pushed to his feet and spotted her standing with his aunt. "Oh, hello."

She couldn't help but smile. Paxton was probably the sweetest of the Farraday brothers. At least the ones she'd met. "Hello."

Just then, Adam leaned in against his aunt, ducking his head close to her ear and softly whispered, "Don't even think about it," before kissing her on the temple and catching up to his wife who was already in the kitchen laughing with several other women.

Not sure what to make of all the muttering, she noticed Owen held what she suspected were the drawings for the hotel. "Any changes?"

Owen's brows lifted. "As a matter of fact, yes."

"Anything I need to know about?" She did her best to sound casual and relaxed, but she hoped she wasn't sneering at him.

"You could say that." Walking past her without a word, he hovered over the coffee table and rolled out the drawings. "Want to see?"

She bobbed her head and hurried beside him. At the office, she'd stood beside Tammy. This was the first chance she had to be close enough to Owen Farraday to smell his cologne. Or was it shampoo. Or soap. Or heaven help her, did the man smell that good on his own?

"What do you think?"

Blinking, she looked down at the page. If he'd said

anything to her, she'd completely missed it focusing on something she shouldn't. Taking another minute to study the sketches, she focused more intently and then faced Owen. "You added another floor?"

He nodded.

Casting her attention to the sketches, she considered the addition. "Suites."

Again, Owen bobbed his head.

"Where are the new numbers for the decorating budget?" She hadn't lifted her attention from the papers in front of her when she realized he wasn't answering. Straightening to her full height and turning to face him, the stone-faced expression told her all she needed to know. "It's not increasing?"

"Some, but not much. We're going to have to trim the fat somewhere else."

Everything in her told her to march out the front door, get in her car, drive back to Oklahoma and tell Harriet she'd had enough. Unfortunately, she had bills to pay and a pantry to keep filled. "Any idea what you want to trim?"

The man shrugged. "That's your department."

She seemed to remember someone mentioning there was a policeman in the family. For a brief moment she wondered how much trouble she'd be in if she knocked him on his arrogant posterior. "When do I get to see the progress?"

"We start work first thing in the morning. You are free to look around any time you want. I'll be heading out to Butler Springs."

"Butler who?"

"That's the closest somewhat big city. I have a meeting with a boutique hotel chain for potential management."

"I see."

"If things go well, your budget might get a little padding and we can avoid another imported chair fiasco."

What an arrogant… If she never had to work another project with this particular Farraday, it wouldn't be soon enough. Though, she couldn't argue about a better budget. Every inch of wiggle room she could squeeze out of this project could only help.

"No more shop talk." Ryan came over and slapped his older brother on the shoulder. "You'll get to do plenty of that with the city council tomorrow."

"Council?" Owen's brows dipped into a deep V.

"Didn't Morgan tell you?

Shaking his head, he blew out a slow heavy sigh. "No."

"They want to see how things are coming along, and want to be walked through the new changes."

"But there's nothing new to see?" Owen's frown grew deeper.

Ryan nudged his brother toward the kitchen. "Which is why you're meeting with them and not me. I'm the hammer and nail guy. No subtlety. You, on the other hand, can sell a man the shirt off his back before he notices he's buying a shirt he already owns."

"I have a meeting with the management company lined up."

Ryan shrugged. "So change it."

"I think the city council will be easier to reschedule. I really need to hit that boutique hotel tomorrow, time is running out."

Connie watched the two politely disagree as they bantered back and forth over the short distance to the kitchen. The three had barely crossed into the room when large bowls of steaming food were shoved into the brothers' hands.

"Dining room," a pretty blonde said before turning her attention from Ryan to Connie. "I'm Joanna, Finn's wife. Nice to meet you."

"Don't dawdle." A redhead who'd passed a dish off to Owen smiled at her. "Things always get a little crazy when the food is ready. I'm Catherine Farraday. Connor belongs to me."

"Nice to meet you. Can I help?"

"Not unless you want Aunt Eileen to shoot us," Joanna laughed. "Guests just eat."

"But go ahead and make yourself comfortable in the dining room. We're going to shoo everyone mulling about in that direction."

"There you are." Eileen Farraday came up to her sporting a grin that could put a scared rabbit at ease. "Why don't you take a seat by me."

Connie followed the matriarch a few feet and sat at the last seat to one end.

"And you sit there." Eileen pointed at the seat next to her. "And you over there." Her hand swung about from Paxton to the other side.

With a short nod, the man did as he was told.

Not till she heard the chair beside her scrape against the floor did she look up to see Owen seated beside her. Somehow she just knew this was about to be the longest dinner of her life.

CHAPTER FIVE

onnie couldn't remember ever having such a sound deep sleep. The bed was better than sleeping on a cloud, and the country quiet was a welcome change. Not to mention the lack of street lamps made it too easy to sleep in. A large to-go cup of coffee in hand, she was out the door.

Having been warned that the town was not recognized by GPS yet, with a detailed map in hand that Meg had given her, she'd made her way out of Tuckers Bluff and was now pulling into her very first, real live—so to speak—ghost town. The first thing to strike her was how clean everything looked. Ridiculously, she realized she was expecting dusty streets with massive balls of tumbleweed blowing about, broken signs hanging from their intended location and flapping about in the blustery breeze, but more so, spur sporting cowboys with handlebar mustaches and pearl handled six shooters should have been roaming the wooden sidewalk.

While there were a handful of contractors moving about, tool belts and power tools replaced visions of cowboys and spurs. There was the one thing she'd gotten right. The entire town, what little of it there was, seemed to be lined with wooden sidewalks. For the first time since she got roped into this project, she was actually feeling excited to be involved.

Focusing at the storefront windows and thinking how much work there was left to do, and not paying attention, her toe caught on the edge of an uplifted board. Carrying her portfolio in one hand and handbag in the other, she flailed forward like a clumsy bear fresh out of hibernation.

A small shrill escaped from her lips seconds before strong hands manacled her upper arms and held her upright.

"Careful." The low deep voice flamed the adrenaline rushing through every cell.

Tamping down the embarrassment at being such a distracted klutz, she sucked in a deep breath and straightened her shoulders, thankful she hadn't broken a shoe or worse, her neck. "Thank…" the sight of Owen Farraday staring down at her, his eyes filled with something that seemed very much like concern, almost robbed her of all rational thought. "Thank you."

His grip loosened, but he remained close, too close, his hands hovering at the ready to steady her once again. "You okay?"

Blinking a few times, she managed to nod and take a single step in retreat. "Yes. I wasn't paying attention. Won't make that mistake again."

"This place is pretty old. There's still a great deal to do to bring this town into the modern millennium. It pays to be careful."

All she could do was bob her head. How had she not noticed the deep timbre of his voice before? Oh yeah, normally he wasn't worried about her, he was grumbling at her. She took another step back and reminded herself that she didn't particularly care for this man. Giving herself a mental shake, she glanced across the street toward all the activity and pointed. "I'm guessing that's the hotel."

"It is." This time he took a step back. "I was just on my way to get some coffee for the crew. How do you take yours?"

She came within an inch of saying no thank you, except the idea of a second cup of morning brew made her want to coo with delight. "Milk and one sugar."

"Got it." Her gaze followed him down the sidewalk and around the bend to where a food truck was parked.

Tearing her eyes away from him before the man noticed she was looking, she took in the building across the street and pushed forward. As she crossed the street, the original front doors drew her in. Dark wood, with glazed glass and gold hotel lettering added a new level of charm to the town. That spark of enthusiasm that had been slowly stirring inside her was now gurgling to the surface.

Inside, the organized chaos was in complete opposition to the quaint wooden walkway and gilded doors. Chalky dust covered absolutely everything. Inching her way toward the original check-in counter, she swept her hand over the dust covered mahogany trim and sighed. Someone should have had the good sense to cover this thing before construction began. The small piece would not be enough to create a modern lobby, but preservation was key to atmosphere.

"Morning." Ryan came trotting down the wide wooden steps and smiled at her. "Great, isn't it?" The man's enthusiasm was infectious.

"I'd like to try and save some of these original pieces." Her hand rubbed over the dusty banister.

"Then you're going to love the pieces stored in the building next door."

"Really?" Her curiosity was piqued.

"Would I shi…lie to you?"

Another worker came up and interrupted, asking about paint colors. Her mind scrambled. She'd been given the impression the project was just beginning. That the camera crews had yet to arrive. Why were they talking paint before she'd even had a chance to draw mockups and put color charts together?

"Coffee call." Owen's voice carried through the small lobby as he appeared with a tray of coffee cups. Any thoughts of color charts and paint colors and timetables fell out her ears.

Anyone would have thought someone had shot off a starting pistol. Workers came out of the proverbial woodwork, down the stairs, through doorways, a few even came in the front door. Where the heck had they been working?

A warm cup of coffee appeared in front of her. "Here you go. Milk and sugar."

"Thank you." More gingerly than was necessary, she

eased the cup away from him.

With the same speed the crew descended on them, coffee in hand, they disappeared just as quickly.

"Ready for the tour?" Ryan asked.

"Absolutely." She nodded.

"Great. Owen, you show her the rooms upstairs. I have to deal with the elevator guy."

"Do I want to know why?" Owen asked.

Ryan shook his head. "Nope. I'll tell you all about it after I've fixed the mix up."

"Mix up?" Owen rolled his eyes, and Connie could see the sweet stranger who'd brought everyone coffee slip away and Owen the Hun taking his place.

Without another word, they climbed the stairs to the next floor and the floor above that. She walked into the first room and was shocked to find new sheetrock already taped and bedded with new wiring coming out of the socket and switch boxes, waiting for a layer of texture. "Good grief. I thought construction was just starting, not almost finishing."

"Sorry we didn't make it more clear. Only a few rooms were saved for filming demolition and construction. While the A crew films that, another will be filming the work in the public areas."

"What about the penthouse suites?"

Owen sighed. "That may pose a problem. I'll have to wait till the film crew gets here. I honestly have no idea."

"Well," she glanced around at the surrounding walls, "I'd better get with my sources and see what supplies we can get here sooner than later."

"About that."

She didn't like the sound of how he'd said that.

"One of the stipulations for this project is that all materials used have to be sourced locally."

"There's a locally around here?" The wording made no sense, but Owen knew what she meant. This ghost town clearly didn't have a surplus supply or tile shop and Tuckers Bluff was a bona fide town, but she doubted there were a whole lot of lighting and tiles stores there either.

"Most everything we'll need can be had in Butler Springs."

"Then I guess we're going to Butler Springs."

"We?" His brows rose high enough to practically kiss his hairline.

She had to admit, when this guy wasn't grumbling or scolding her, he was rather sweet. "Unless there's someone else around here who can show me your sources now, then as soon as you have your meeting with the council, *tag you're it.*"

"Come and gone. This is ranch country and most of the city council are ranchers. Early risers. Business is finished." Owen had no idea how he'd drawn the short stick, but the last thing he wanted to do right now was take a long drive in the confinement of his truck cab with a beautiful woman who smelled of vanilla and sweetness. The second he'd reached for her as she went stumbling along the walkway, he knew he was in trouble. Until now, Connie had been nothing more than the brunt of his financial frustrations. A rather stubborn woman with limited understanding of the budget restrictions. Outside on the sidewalk, she was suddenly a delicate, soft, and beautiful woman with dark brown eyes that a man could easily lose his soul to. How the heck had he missed those eyes? And more so, how was he supposed to ignore those same eyes for hours in a confined space?

"Good. The sooner we get started the better. Since we're out in the middle of nowhere Texas, I'm assuming this town isn't around the corner."

"You would be correct."

She flipped her wrist, glancing at her watch. "Will we make it before lunch? Or should I grab something from the food trucks?"

"Yes, and it's up to you."

Her gaze drifted to the food truck that had become a staple for not only the crew, but townsfolk as well would make the long drive for a taste of Molly's cooking. When she bit down and nibbled on her lower lip, Owen couldn't have dragged his gaze away from the way her mouth moved as she considered her choices if someone had offered him all the oil in Texas.

"There will be plenty of time for Molly's cooking if you want to see what the options are in Butler Springs."

Nodding her head, she blew out a soft sigh of decision and turned on her heel. "Good idea. Are we taking my car or yours?"

"Mine. I know where we're going." He was just going to have to toss a few things into the back seat to make room for her. When he'd left the ranch this morning he had not expected to be chauffeuring anyone around the state.

"I really should have worn different shoes." Muttering to herself, she dropped her purse into the front seat, latched onto the grab bar, and hauled herself up and into his truck.

"Sorry. Should have warned you. Out here boots are best. Especially near the tall grass."

Squeezing her eyes shut, she tossed her head back against the seat. "Snakes."

"Affirmative. Not as many as before all the construction began, but this is West Texas."

"Noted." Heaving out a deep sigh, it took another moment before she opened her eyes. "What time is your meeting with the hotel management company?"

"Not till two o'clock."

Her head bobbed and her lips pursed for a long moment, and Owen decided he was going to have to stop looking at her when she was thinking. He liked it better when she ticked him off. These tantalizing gestures were already driving him to distraction.

"You know." She cocked her head and stared at him intently. "Does the hotel have a restaurant?"

He nodded.

"We could have lunch at the hotel. It would allow us an inside look, so to speak, of how they actually manage things."

The idea had merit. He'd even considered booking a room for a weekend to see how well they did for himself.

Not that it should matter to him, he was only on the construction end. But the success of the Three Corners as a serious tourist attraction was important to the town of Tuckers Bluff, its residents, and more importantly, the Farradays, which made this management choice about more than just how much money they would contribute to the project coffers. "Looks like we're having lunch at the boutique hotel."

Having pulled a notebook out of her purse, Connie had spent the better part of the drive making notes. Occasionally, she'd lift her head to glance around at the surroundings or ask him a question. Not till they were at the outskirts of town did she put her notes away and look at her watch. "Do you want to get lunch out of the way? Or shall we hit up some of your sources?"

Looking at the hour on his dashboard, they probably had time for a stop or two first. "Where exactly do you want to go?"

Opening her notebook, she flipped through a few pages and then bobbed her head. "Who's your furniture source? We need to get some options for the lobby and the rooms. I'd also like to see some wallpaper options. A building of that era should have at least some wallpaper. Also a specialty carpet company would be good. Then I need fixtures for the bathrooms." Tapping the paper, she paused for a deep breath. "We'll need hardware too, and—"

He held his hand up. "I think we've got more than enough there. You're going to need more than an afternoon for all that."

"I will, but we have to start somewhere."

"We'll go to the furniture store first. It's closer to the hotel."

Nodding, she did that nibble on her lower lip thing and Owen decided that this was going to be a very, very long day.

CHAPTER SIX

Not in her entire life had Connie done so much work in a moving car. The truth was, ever since tumbling into Owen's arms back at the ghost town, she forgot about the bossy penny pincher and kept thinking about the feel of those strong arms steadying her on her feet. The last thing she wanted was to spend the drive looking at the barren brown land surrounding them, or deep blue eyes the color of the Texas sky.

Another few minutes and they pulled into the parking lot in front of a small cinder block building painted white with a shiny metal roof. "This is the furniture store?"

Owen nodded and unbuckled his seat belt. "They have a pretty little store downtown, but this is the heart of the operation."

From where she stood, the heart of this operation looked like it was in need of a good cardiologist.

Holding the door open for her, Connie nodded and crossed the threshold. She should know by now that appearances could be deceiving. From the outside the place didn't look like much more than an oversized garage, but inside, she was reminded that everything is bigger in Texas. "Whoa." She dared steal a glance in Owen's direction in time to catch him grinning like the cat who'd swallowed the proverbial canary. Yep, the cocky know-it-all she'd known all this time was back.

A wiry older man crossed the massive showroom floor. "Mr. Farraday. How can we help you?"

"Call me Owen, please."

The old man nodded. "What are we looking for? Building more homes?"

"Well, yes we are, but that's not what we're here for."

Holding up one finger, the man's toothy grin spread. "The hotel. It's time."

"It is." Owen turned to face Connie. "This is the designer extraordinaire in charge. Be nice to her."

Connie actually did a double take. She supposed that might be the closest thing to a compliment she'd hear from Owen.

"What do we want?"

Owen pointed to a large sofa in a paisley print with multiple cushion backing. "This looks comfy."

"Maybe, but we need durable first, so leather. Also, no one wants to sit between two people. Especially if they're strangers. We'll do loveseats. And club chairs. Wing backs would be nice."

Owen's brows buckled creating a deep ridge above his nose.

"Are you looking for a particular style?" The old man spoke as he moved diagonally across the space.

"Traditional. Rolled arms. Rounded feet. Not too large."

Nodding the old man kept walking. "Simple enough."

The three of them perused the different options. A few came close, but she was searching for just the right style to draw modern comfort together with hundred plus year old construction. In the end, she took photos of a maybe sofa set. "Where are the beds and mattresses?"

Turning his wrist to look at his watch as he'd done maybe a hundred times in the short time they'd been there, Owen didn't say a word, but followed behind her as they crossed the massive warehouse hidden behind the tiny concrete building visible from the parking lot.

"Here you go." The older man smiled and waved an arm. "I'm afraid I have some business to tend to, but if you find the set you want just take note of the model number on this tag and let Jane at the front desk know how many you want and when you need them delivered."

Connie nodded and slowly strolled through the sea of beds taking note of pillow tops, double sided, and firmness grade.

"Good grief." Owen scanned the expansive area filled with puffy white display beds. "Has anyone ever heard of overkill?"

"Nonsense. Mattresses are a big deal. A good night's sleep will do more for the hotel's reputation than anything else."

"I don't know about that. No one has coined the phrase the way to a man's heart is through a good mattress."

Connie rolled her eyes. "Maybe not in so many words."

The way Owen's eyes widened and his brows shot up to his hairline as it dawned on him how that simple change of the old cliché about a man's stomach could easily be misunderstood almost had her spitting with laughter. "I didn't mean…"

She raised her hand. "I know. All you Farradays are as polite and well mannered as the day is long. If there were a puddle in here, you'd probably lay your coat down over it and carry me across."

The comment was meant as jab at the extreme, but Owen merely smiled and nodded with a glint of pride in his eyes. "My mama would be very happy to hear you say that."

"Come on." She walked toward one queen size mattress that had caught her eye. The moment she sat, she sank into a hefty amount of padding and shrugged. Laying down she didn't quite feel like sleeping on a cloud, but she was comfortable.

"Is that it? How much does it cost?"

"Always the money man." She patted the mattress. "Lay down. You tell me."

"I don't think that will be—"

"Just lay down."

Heaving out a deep breath, he flopped on the bed with such force, her feet bounced up, her arms flew out, and she almost rolled off the other side.

"I don't think so," Connie said.

"Why? It feels fine. How much is it?"

"It's only fine if the hotel doesn't care about being sued if someone rolls off and breaks an arm or their neck."

With those words he sprang up and extended an arm to help her up. "Which one now?"

The penny pincher had slipped away, hidden behind the chivalrous, sparkling blue eyes of an irresistible gentleman. If she knew what was good for her, she'd get up on her own steam. Then again, who said she knew what was good for her?

The second Connie's slim fingers curled around his hand, he second guessed his own choices. She was neither the first nor last woman on the planet he would offer a hand to assist climbing out of a car, onto a step, or up from a comfortable resting place, and yet, something deep in his gut didn't want to let go. Simply because of the strong urge to walk around the store holding her hand like a teen on his first date, he pulled his hand back quickly. Almost too quickly. "After you."

"I'm looking for mattresses that can be flipped. They'll last longer."

He nodded at her though to be honest, he'd never paid that much attention to mattress construction, and frankly, had no clue if growing up his parents flipped their mattresses or not. He certainly had never thought to do so.

"This one looks good." She pressed the top with her hand. "We'll want Queen for the regular rooms, but King for the suites."

Already knowing the plan, he walked around the foot of the bigger bed and once again, flopped onto the mattress like a man who had run the seven minute mile in five minutes. Connie apparently had the same idea. The two collapsed heavily onto the bed, bounced, only this time, whatever supported the massive mattress gave out underneath and the two rolled smack into each other.

If he thought touching hands was risky business, having Connie up close and very personal was testing that chivalry his mother so patiently instilled in him.

"Having fun?" the older voice asked.

Arms flailing, the two scrambled to separate, the awkward angle of the collapsed middle had them making a smidge of progress only to fall right back into each other. He'd had less trouble crawling out of an old fashioned water bed than they were having scrambling off the broken bed.

On her hands and knees, Connie crawled to the edge and rolled over, landing on the floor with a thud.

"Oh dear." The old man frowned. No doubt thoughts of lawsuits running through his head. "I'm so sorry. Arthur must have forgotten the middle support."

Scooting to the bottom until his booted feet hit the floor, Owen sprang upright and hurried around to where Connie still sat on the floor, leaning against the bed. He'd expected to find a furious and possibly injured decorator. Instead her chest heaved not racked with tears, but holding back laughter.

"I think," she chuckled a bit more loudly, "we should skip the shopping and just have lunch."

"I really am sorry." The old man hovered by their side as Connie pushed to her feet.

"No harm, no foul," Connie reassured the man.

Owen took a few minutes to add his reassurances to the business owner and escorted Connie back to the truck. A few more minutes down the main drag and they pulled into the boutique hotel parking lot.

In front, Connie stared up at the façade. "Nice old building."

"Not as old as ours."

She shook her head. "No, it's not."

Together they entered the main lobby and crossed the small art deco area to the glass doors that led to the restaurant. The plans for the ghost town hotel would do the same thing. The restaurant could be reached through the entrance to what was once the saloon, or from the lobby of the hotel. The two buildings side by side, it made sense to absorb the saloon. They'd already connected the former upstairs 'social' rooms next door to the main hotel with a new hallway. The addition, thanks to Neil's skills, turned out seamless. They'd consider making that part of the TV show, but in the end, decided to just do it and move on.

The restaurant had the same Art Deco vibe as the lobby.

Connie leaned in and lowered her voice. "I feel like someone vomited the Great Gatsby all over this room. I'm all for black and gold but this is just a bit much."

He had to admit that he agreed with her. The in your face décor was not what he'd expected.

Holding a menu, the hostess smiled up at them. "Two?"

They both nodded and followed her to a large two top table by the windows near the rear of the establishment.

"This is nice." Owen appreciated the size of the table. "Nothing worse than not having enough room on the table for food and drinks.

Connie frowned and Owen wondered what was going through her mind.

"Something wrong?" he asked.

She bobbed her head. "Actually, yes. I'm with you in thinking that the tabletop is a good size, but..."

"But?"

"Cross your legs."

"Excuse me?"

"Go ahead. Cross your legs."

He did as instructed and immediately understood the dilemma. The table was too low for him to cross his legs comfortably. "I'm taller than the average man."

"But I'm not and I've banged my knee twice already in less than five minutes."

"So we'd want higher tables."

"We would." She blew out a small sigh and focused her gaze on him. "But what really has me confused is why did these tables ever wind up here in the first place. Was their decorator a ten year old?"

The vision made him chuckle. He could just see a short, bossy little kid with a clipboard ordering grown men around.

For the next few minutes they studied the menu while she critiqued the rough fabric on the chairs that tugged at her dress and put forth more than one concern about how the management would translate for the vision the brothers, cousin, and town had for their little project.

"All you have to do is look at any of your faces when you talk about the project to know how much y'all really love what you're doing."

"My poor father wishes it weren't so. As we grew up and moved in different directions, the ranch became smaller and smaller until Dad finally had to give up on the idea of the ranch passing on to any of us."

"Is that how the Christmas tree farm came to be?"

Owen nodded. "It is."

"You're smiling."

"Excuse me?"

"You've got that look of someone with a secret."

His smile grew brighter. "Just going down memory lane. We all thought Dad was insane when he suggested the idea to my mother."

"She wasn't onboard?"

"Mom's rarely onboard with much of anything. Don't get me wrong, she's a great woman and a loving mother, but if you want to know why something is wrong, difficult, or inappropriate, ask my mother for her opinion. Though when Morgan and Neil told her they wanted to start their own construction business, that was probably the first time ever that I can remember where Mom didn't have an objection."

"Well, that's good." Connie snapped her napkin open and laid it on her lap. "Are you and your brothers as close as it looks to outsiders?"

Again, he nodded. "Pretty much. Though of course, I'm closest to Pax. Paxton. I suppose when you're a twin there's no avoiding that underlying connection. Even more so when you're identical."

"I've actually always thought it would be fun to have a twin. Especially when I need to be two places at once."

"I bet." He couldn't help but chuckle at the river of memories that came to mind. As little kids they were constantly confusing their teachers and playing tricks on friends. Of course it made it so much easier that their mother insisted on sending them to elementary school in matching clothes.

"Oh. You're not only smiling wider, there's a new sparkle in your eyes. Penny for your thoughts."

"It's the two places at once comment. Every once in a while that actually worked out for us. Sort of."

"Sort of?" her eyes widened and the corner of her lips tipped upward.

He really did like her smile. "The first time it backfired on us was our junior year of high school. Pax accidentally made two dates for the same night."

"Accidentally?"

"That's what he said. He'd worked for months to get Patty Nelson to say yes to a date and then in his enthusiasm, he'd forgotten he already had promised Maggie Roberti that he'd escort her to her brother's wedding the same day. He needed me to step in for him."

"So which one did you take out?"

"Maggie, of course. Pax wasn't letting anyone near Patty."

"So what went wrong?"

"Nothing. Until after the wedding. Even though Pax and I are totally different—"

"How so?"

He shrugged. "Different temperaments mostly. Though Pax is a fantastic cook. For a while there we thought he was going to be a professional chef. I, on the other hand, can burn water."

"That bad?" She laughed.

"Pretty much. Anyhow, despite our differences, we know each other extremely well. Sometimes we know more about our sibling than we do about ourselves. Pretending to be each other was something we'd done well since we were knee high to a grasshopper."

"Well, something had to happen for the effort to only sort of work."

"To my surprise, I was actually having a nice time with Maggie, and I think she was having fun too. But when the wedding ended she was hungry so we went to the Broad

Street Diner for a midnight snack."

Connie winced.

"Yep. Great minds think alike because Pax had taken Patty there for a late night snack too."

"Busted." Connie smiled and shook her head. "Serves you both right for trying to fool the women."

"Yep. In the end neither girl would talk to either of us."

"Good for them. At least you learned your lesson."

He did his best to bite back a smile, but Connie called him out on it.

"You're grinning again. Don't tell me you did it again?"

"Okay." He casually shrugged his shoulders. "I won't tell you."

That brought the first real belly laugh from Connie. The sound was infectious. Within minutes, they were both laughing to the point of tears. He could almost imagine how she'd react at some of their other stories. Of course, there were a few that were simply going to have to stay locked behind closed lips. Though he wouldn't have thought this a few days ago, right now he didn't want to do anything to chase Connie away. What he had to decide now was did he want to do anything to bring Connie closer?

CHAPTER SEVEN

"So, what did you think?" Owen pulled the truck door shut behind him.

While Owen had visited with the management team at the boutique hotel, Connie had looked around the rest of the hotel. With the hotel manager's permission, one of the housekeepers gave her access to a regular guest room and a suite. For her taste, the mattresses were overly firm, but she understood that the more firm a mattress was the longer its lifespan in a situation like a hotel. By the time Connie and Owen were finished at the hotel, the day had gotten away from them and they needed to return to Tuckers Bluff.

Connie slipped the seat belt into place, and tired of walking in heels, kicked her shoes off. "Not bad, but nothing special. What about you?"

He gave a soft chuckle. "Not bad, but nothing special."

Throwing her own words back at her had been annoying, but his smile told her he truly felt the same way she had. "Are they a contender?"

He blew out a heavy sigh. "Maybe, but I don't think so. They said all the right things, but it didn't really resonate."

"Good choice of words. I felt the same way walking through the hotel. There was nothing special, nothing to endear me, nothing that made me feel special or enticed me to want to come back someday. And that is not what I thought you guys wanted for the new hotel."

"You're right. The whole town is excited about all that is coming together with the ghost town. Not only are they enjoying bringing the history back to life, and the attention of the TV show, but the potential for a new community and all that comes with it has everyone involved. The longer we work on bringing this old town back to life, the more my brothers and I feel the same way."

"So far, from what I've seen, y'all are doing a good job."

"Heaven knows I'm getting a crash course in hotel management." He turned to face her and smiled more widely. "And design."

His phone rang and he pushed the button on the steering wheel for the car to answer. "Owen here."

"Mr. Farraday, this is Kathy. I wanted to confirm the final headcount for the buses."

"I'm sorry. I'm on the road and don't have access to that. I thought we had another week before you needed the numbers?"

"You do, but I have a last minute request to book some buses for a wedding and don't want to leave you short."

"I see. Can I get back to you tomorrow with some numbers?"

"Of course."

He said his goodbyes, and then called his brother.

"What's up, bro?"

"The bus company wants a final headcount, something about needing buses for a wedding. Do you think the numbers we have are all we're going to need?"

"We didn't tell everyone they had an early deadline to participate. I can make some phone calls and see if there's any possibility that we'll have last-minute sign-ups."

"That would be good. I think we should probably overestimate. I don't want to turn away anyone who wants to participate."

"Agreed. As Mom used to say, in for a penny, in for a pound. This is costing us a small fortune anyhow, what's a little bit more?" The deep voice on the other end chuckled.

"It'll be worth it. All that matters is that the kids –as many kids as possible—have a great time. We can make more money another day."

"Should I talk to Valerie and see if the network would like to sponsor some of this?"

Now she realized he was talking to Morgan. She also realized there was definitely another side to the Scrooge at Farraday Construction Company.

"Not really. Granted, it would be nice to have extra money to spend, but I really don't want to deal with network red tape and who knows what other obstacles. Let's just do this the way we want to. Don't you think?"

"I agree with you. Will I see you at the ranch for dinner tonight?"

"Not sure yet."

"Fair enough. Talk to you later."

From that point on, the phone didn't stop. No wonder the guy had a tendency to be grumpy. Everybody who called brought one challenge after another and Owen seemed to be the fixit man for all of it. From what she could gather there was a problem with a real estate deal they were involved in. She'd had no idea that Owen also held a real estate license. There was another issue with a special order of some wood she had never heard of for a project in northern Oklahoma. And if that wasn't enough, there was a break-in at a remodeling project where the thieves tore out all the walls to cut out copper. She knew she'd worked with the brothers on different projects, but had not realized just how far spread their operation was. At one point his Aunt Eileen called to inform him that he was bringing Connie to dinner at the ranch and one of his cousins would take her back to town, then Owen could pick her up in the morning to take her to the ghost town for her car.

"Yes, ma'am. I'll check if she's all right with that plan." He glanced at Connie and she shrugged. She had a feeling from the tone in his aunt's voice and all the stories that she had heard that there wouldn't be any point in her objecting anyhow. "That'll be fine, Aunt Eileen."

The tone of the conversation shifted, and a tenderness could be heard in both Owen and his aunt's voice. This family really was something special. And just like the rest of the drive, a call came in and Owen politely cut his aunt off and took the call from a brother with another problem to resolve. Apparently she'd underestimated Mr. Owen

Farraday and would have to work on cutting the guy a little slack. Maybe.

A constantly ringing phone was a fact of life for Owen, but this was ridiculous. He'd barely gotten a chance to share two words with Connie. He'd wanted to hear more of her thoughts, especially if the brief shopping trip had helped. Usually sourcing projects was relatively simple, and much could be done online, but this project was a bit more unique than their usual fare.

Not till he pulled onto the drive on his aunt and uncle's property was he finally able to end the last call and tired, tossed his phone into the glove compartment. "It's quitting time."

The moment he opened the door, Gray ran up to the truck. His tail wagging against the dirt, the dog waited patiently for him to lean over and scratch behind his ears. "And how are you doing?"

Gray gave a single happy bark, while his cohort scurried around to the passenger side.

"Well, aren't you a sweetie," Connie mimicked Owen, leaning over and scratching the scruff of the patient dog's neck.

"It's about time y'all got here." Leaning against a post on the porch, his aunt smiled at them. "Don't dawdle. Everyone's starving."

"Yes, ma'am." He patted the top of Gray's head and nodding at his aunt as she turned into the house, he walked side by side with Connie to the porch and into the house.

"Do you guys do this a lot?" Connie paused to give the dogs sitting on the porch one last stroke.

"This what?"

"Gather for dinner. I mean, I know Sunday is a big deal. But it's a week night and not like y'all live next door."

"Technically Connor does. And Finn is on the property. But there won't be a big crowd on a Monday night. Mostly it will be those of us staying here.”

"I see.”

“Uncle Owen, look what I did!” Connor's daughter came running up waving a piece of paper at him.

Squatting down to level his gaze with hers, he reached for the paper. “Oh my. What a beautiful painting.”

Eyes twinkling with delight, the little girl beamed up at him. “It's your horse.”

“It looks just like Brady.” To his surprise, the simple painting looked like it could be any horse, but it was very definitely a well-defined horse. Proportioned properly, he suspected Stacey was going to be quite the artist some day.

“Mommy says I can sit by you at dinner if it's okay with you?”

“Of course it is. How about a special ride to the dining room?”

The little girl flashed a bright toothy grin and bobbed her head feverishly.

“Off we go, princess.” Owen lifted his niece off the floor, twirled her around, and then sat her on his shoulders. “Your meal awaits, your highness.”

Stacey giggled, and Owen thanked the Lord for reuniting the Oklahoma Farradays with the Texas branch of the family. Small children around always brightened a day. For some reason, Stacey had taken a liking to him the first time they met. Her love of horses came naturally being raised on a horse ranch, but she seemed to have a special way with animals. Brady had bruised a hoof on a stone and little Stacey had spoken to the horse in a soothing tone that kept him calm while Owen tended to the irritation. From that moment on, whenever possible, Brady followed the little girl around like a lost puppy. The sight was amazing, such a huge animal and such a dainty little girl made for a picture perfect view and was the cornerstone to making him, at least for now, her favorite uncle. He suspected that soon he'd be dethroned by another Farraday, but until then he intended to enjoy the special attentions bestowed on him.

At the table Stacey sat to one side and Aunt Eileen sat Connie at the other.

"How did you like Butler Springs?" Catherine, Stacey's mom, asked Connie.

"Didn't really get to see much of it."

Morgan reached for the bread dish. "Sounds like we need to come up with a different option for managing the hotel when the project is done."

"Connie pointed out a few things that the boutique operation missed the mark on and even though we're in charge of presenting a turn key hotel so the chairs won't scratch and the patrons won't knock knees with the tables, I didn't see the attention to detail we're going for."

Neil nodded. "We have options. Tomorrow I'll follow up on a few."

"Sounds like a plan."

"Speaking of which." Valerie set her fork on the dish. "While you were in Butler Springs the TV crew set up to start filming. We've been handed a new schedule from the network and unless we get some extra hammers onboard, we're not going to be able to keep up."

Valerie was a reality show producer extraordinaire, and after several episodes of the Construction Cousins show, she'd become pretty darn good at making the filming schedule and construction schedule work together.

"There's no way we can pull any more crew off other projects." Quinn shook his head.

"Which means," Neil waved a fork in the air, "we pencil pushers get to put on a tool belt. Again."

Tapping her nose with her finger, Valerie nodded.

"It'll be fun," Morgan added. "Look how well the homestead project went."

Pax dipped his head to one side. "If you don't count Owen putting his foot through the ceiling."

"Let's not go there," Owen sighed. His mom had finally put two and two together about the big ghost town production and the Farradays of Tuckers Bluff and had been blowing up his phone that day. Between the constant distraction and the dark attic, a single misstep and he'd been practically dangling from the rafters.

"You fell through the ceiling?" Connie's rounded eyes

resembled a startled owl.

"Just my foot."

Her gaze remained filled with surprise.

"Oh," Aunt Eileen waved a hand at Connie, "I almost forgot to tell you. I ran into the Sisters when I was in town this afternoon and they said to let you know they have a few items left over from when they redid the bordello…"

Connie leaned into him and softly asked, "Did she just say bordello?"

Chuckling softly, Owen nodded.

"…and they thought you might be able to use some of it at the hotel. They also said to let you know that they have some wonderful online sources."

Connie nodded. "Thank you. But who are the sisters?"

"Oh. Sorry. I forgot you're not from around here." Aunt Eileen rolled her eyes at her own mistake. "They own the general store downtown. It's called Sisters."

"I see." Connie nodded.

"I'll take you over to meet them," DJs wife, Becky, volunteered. "I have to pick up a pair of new shoes I ordered for Katie. They light up and I thought she'd enjoy that."

"I'll have to get my car tomorrow morning and take some measurements, but when I get back to town, I would love the introduction."

"And on that note," Becky picked up her and her husband's dinner plate, "I have to pick Katie up from Meg and Adam's, so it's time for us to say goodnight."

Connie pushed back from the table. "I'll gather my purse. I really appreciate the lift."

"Our pleasure." DJ took hold of his wife's hand and grinned down at her before casting a softer smile on Connie.

Even though DJ was extremely happily married, for some odd reason Owen found himself wanting to growl at his cousin, telling him to keep his smile to himself. How crazy was that?

CHAPTER EIGHT

"What do you think of Tuckers Bluff so far?" Meg set a dish of fresh baked goods in front of Connie.

Most of her life, Connie thought there was no waking up till she'd had her second cup of coffee. Apparently a good whiff of Toni's baked goods could do the same. "I need to explore a little more. Visit the Sisters, but the ghost town is seriously cool. Not sure what I expected but I was very impressed."

"We all are having fun with it. Ever since Joanna discovered the connection between Three Corners and Tuckers Bluff and the Sisters, we were intrigued. When the production company got involved and started helping restore the old town, we've become totally enthralled. I, for one, can't wait to see the final product."

"Ditto." Becky walked in the door. "I can hardly wait for the hotel and spa to open and turn our Friday night girls' night into a weekend stay."

"Good morning." The voice coming down the hall was deep, throaty, decidedly male, and to her surprise, she knew exactly who it was.

"This is a surprise." Meg smiled at her husband's cousin as he entered the kitchen.

Taking a moment to hug both Becky and Meg, Owen shrugged. "Sissy called and said the costumes are in for the Palooza so Aunt Eileen sent me to pick them up, and while I'm here, give Connie a lift to the worksite to retrieve her car."

"Oh good." Becky reached for a croissant. "I'd have gladly taken her, but if you're going that way anyhow,

Adam will be happy to see me at work sooner than later."

"Are you ready to go?" Owen faced Connie.

She bobbed her head, slung her purse over her shoulder, and grabbed another muffin. "Ready."

"Wait." Meg held her hand and poured coffee into a to-go cup along with the right amount of sugar and milk. No wonder the woman was a great innkeeper, she remembered everything.

"Thanks."

"Okay. We're off. Catch y'all later." Owen gestured for Connie to go ahead, then held the front door for her. The entire Farraday clan really was a throwback to an age of chivalry that Connie thought had been eroded beyond recovery.

"Sisters is just down the hill and around the corner on Main Street. It will only take a minute to get there." Owen closed her door behind her and circled the hood.

Once he was in his car, she asked, "What costumes are you picking up?"

"For the Palooza."

"I've heard that a few times already. What exactly is the Palooza?"

"It's a weekend event at the ghost town for underprivileged kids in foster care."

Honestly she had no idea what the Palooza was for, but if she had, this would not have been on her radar.

"Back home, as time permitted, we helped out with mentoring programs. Here in Tuckers Bluff we are isolated from the larger problem. DJ mentioned that a social worker in Butler Springs was telling him the challenges they were facing with an overburdened caseload. One Sunday after church the family got to talking, we consider doing a special ranchathon for fosters—"

"I'm sorry, ranchathon?"

Owen chuckled. "That's like a mini family rodeo that Uncle Sean and Aunt Eileen do at the ranch every year. But somehow the idea shifted from an afternoon at the ranch to a weekend at the ghost town. It will be two days and two nights. The shops that are up and running will be manned by town folk in full costume. We're going to clean up the saloon enough to put on a show for them. We'll set up tents for sleeping, have a nighttime campfire with ghost stories and marshmallow roasting and just enjoying the blanket of stars that this part of the country gets. A lot of these kids have no idea how beautiful the night sky can be when it's not competing with light pollution."

"When is all this happening?"

"Just shy of three weeks."

"Does this have something to do with those buses you were talking about yesterday?"

He nodded. "Yep, and we don't want anyone left out."

This whole thing certainly gave her food for thought. There's polite, well-mannered old-fashioned families, and then there's people who go the extra mile to make a difference. She wasn't sure she ever met both in a single-family.

Owen parked in front of an average size storefront with a big sign overhead that said Sisters. When they opened the front door, an old-fashioned bell sounded notifying the storekeepers that they had customers. Connie wasn't sure what surprised her more, the unexpected size of the interior of the shop compared to the small windows out front, or the two women who appeared from behind the curtain, both dressed in floor length gingham dresses with lace and drop sleeves that looked straight out of an episode of *Gunsmoke* or *Bonanza*. The astonishing part though wasn't the outfits, it was the women themselves. One was extremely tall and thin with red hair, the other was as wide as she was tall with teased blonde hair that gave a whole new meaning to Texas big hair.

"Oh, welcome." The short blonde held the edge of her skirt in each hand and whirled in place. "Are these just wonderful?"

"How fun!" Connie reached out and fingered the skirt of one of the sisters. "I've always thought it would have been fun to have lived in a different era when ordinary clothes were so much more."

"We have plenty of extras. The whole town is interested

in participating in costume to help with the food and carnival games as well as the gunfights and the cattle drive. Would you like to try one on?"

"I'm sorry. Did you say gunfight?"

Owen let out a deep laugh. "Nothing dangerous. Two old coots are going to pretend to have a gunfight on the main street. And the cattle drive will just be a few head of cattle coming down the street and then led into the old stables for the wagon trains."

Connie fingered a dress the tall redhead held out for her. It was fancier than the simple gingham the ladies wore.

"It will look lovely on you," the shorter one encouraged.

"Which reminds me." The tall one snapped her fingers. "We have the vests for the men too. The extra hat orders for the kids will be here in a few days."

"Great. Do I pay you for the hats now?"

The redhead shook her head. "You can pay for them when you pick them up. Now, young lady." The woman spun about and gestured over her shoulder for Connie to follow. "This dress is perfect for you. The whole town is so excited about this event. Those Oklahoma boys are something else, but Owen, he's a real gem."

She wasn't sure about the gem part, but she was starting to figure out there was a lot more to this man than numbers on the spreadsheet.

"I mean, everyone is chipping in something or other. The proceeds from the mercantile we already rehabbed for the show, some of the money from the production company, but what that wouldn't cover, the Farradays stepped up to make sure everything is perfect for those kids. Even the cowboy hats for over fifty children, those are not cheap, and young Owen there is paying for those himself."

Even though Owen stood in the shop on the other side of the curtain, she still looked over her shoulder as if she could see the man the redhead was talking about. Somehow footing the bill for cowboy hats for all those children didn't line up with the grouchy, budget conscious, penny pincher she'd come to know. From the conversation she'd overheard the other day and now what the Sisters were saying about the hats, Connie had a feeling Owen was the one coughing up the money for the extra buses too. It made her wonder.

"Here you go." The redhead opened a narrow door.

Stepping into the dressing room, she stared at the dress the redhead had placed on a hook. "I always loved playing dress up as a kid, but this is a whole new level."

"We discussed ordering shoes to match, but in the end everyone decided our cowboy boots would be well hidden and more sensible. Do you have a pair?"

Connie shook her head, but she had a feeling by the time she left the shop today, she was going to have both a new dress and boots, and a whole lot to think about regarding one Owen Farraday.

While Connie was inside with Sissy trying on the new dress, Sister wrapped and packaged the dress order for the ladies at the ranch the same as if they'd been shopping one hundred and fifty years ago. No shopping bag. Folded and wrapped in brown paper and tied with twine. When Connie came out from behind the curtain, he felt as though he'd been transported back in time. It took everything in him not to gape and mutter something stupid like *wow*. "That dress looks lovely on you."

Her smile was the widest he'd ever seen, she did a cute little shudder with her shoulders and then twirled for him. "I'm told I need cowboy boots too."

"We considered using the fashions from the late 1860s that would have included bustles but in the end the women decided we would have enough to get used to with all the crinolines and bell sleeves."

The dress was a beautiful shade of blue that reflected the dark shade of her eyes. Frilly lace edged the seams and a pretty floral coordinating fabric wrapped around the hips and draped down over the basic blue. Had this really been the late 1800s her family would have been beating off suitors with a stick.

He wasn't sure what came over him, but placing one hand across his stomach and the other hand behind his back, he bowed at the waist. "May I have this dance?"

The lightest shade of pink flushed briefly into her cheeks. Still smiling, she gave a bit of the curtsy. "Thank you, kind sir."

Out of the corner of his eye he barely caught a glimpse Sister gleefully rubbing her hands together, and Sissy rushing behind the counter. A moment later the soft music that played for customers shopping pleasure grew much louder. Although the popular 70s tune was unlike anything like what was played one hundred years prior, he took hold of her hand and proceeded to glide across the floor in his best effort at a Viennese waltz.

The overhead bell of the shop door sounded announcing someone had come in, but he was having too much fun to stop dancing. The next thing he knew, his cousin Adam was dancing with Sissy beside him. Before the end of the song, a few others had come in to pick up their costumes and the echoing of the words one, two, three, one, two, three, could be heard as everyone spun about the shop, now waltzing to another out of date tune.

"Good grief." Frank, the cook from the café, voice boomed. "Have you all lost your minds?"

Pretty much everyone in the shop broke out laughing. Owen reluctantly took a step back, and bowing his head briefly at Connie, smiled. "Thank you."

Beside him, Sister slapped her hands together and practically bounced in her shoes. "I know the Palooza is for the children, but we really should have a little band with some dancing for the adults."

Owen shrugged. While the idea had merit, Sister was correct in that the entire purpose for the event is for the kids not the adults. "Maybe."

"I guess I'd better go change out of this dress." Connie took a step back.

"If you're heading back to Sadieville, you better buy

those boots now." Sister smiled at her.

"Good idea." She scurried behind the curtain.

Adam slapped his cousin on the back. "Well, I have to admit, when Meg asked me to come pick up our costumes, I had no idea I'd be practicing my cotillion classes."

"Well, I, for one, am delighted." Sissy placed her hand on her chest. "It's been a lifetime since I danced with a good-looking young man."

"You really thinking of having a dance at the Palooza?" Adam asked.

"Don't know." He was going to have to talk with his brothers. The whole thing was a family effort.

"I guess I'm all ready." Connie came out of the dressing room and handed the dress to Sister. "I'll take the dress and these boots you picked out are perfect."

For a few more minutes while the Sisters rang Connie up, Owen chatted with Adam and the others who were all waiting patiently to pay for their purchases. From the amount of enthusiasm the town showed, he was willing to bet if the event turned out to be a success that the Palooza might easily turn into a yearly thing.

"So," Connie tossed her new dress, along with her old shoes, into the back seat of his truck and climbed in. "Do you think there's anything I can do to help with this event?"

"You want to help with the Palooza?"

"Don't look so surprised." She chuckled. "I like kids too."

"Too?"

She shrugged. "I could tell by the way you played with your niece last night that you like kids."

He bobbed his head. "I do. They really are a treasure to enjoy."

"Except maybe when they're awake every two hours to be fed for the first nine months of their lives."

"That sounds like the voice of experience. Do you have kids?" There's been no ring on her finger, no mention of a husband left behind, but in today's world, none of that necessarily meant anything.

"Nope. But I have two sisters and three nieces. I adore

them. But my poor sisters were the walking dead the first few months after each baby. And that was with their husband's help. So what can I do?"

"Depends on how dirty you want to get."

"Excuse me?" Her eyebrows shot up high and he bit back a smile at how adorable she looked every time she did that.

"Some of the places we'll be using like the old stables, the saloon, the blacksmith shop, won't have been refurbished, but we need to make sure they're safe as well as cleaned up. Now that the days are longer, we'll be working on it after quitting time. Probably weekends too."

"I'm pretty handy with a mop and a hammer. Count me in."

There was no stopping his face from sporting a huge grin. Whether it was because she wanted to help, or that she knew her way around a toolbox, he didn't know for sure. But whatever the case might be, the next few weeks were looking much brighter.

CHAPTER NINE

So far this morning, Connie had measured the rooms and made a to scale sketch of the three different room options as well as the bathrooms. Purchasing items for the bathrooms was easiest because the configuration of the room had little to do with towels and shower curtains. It was the sleeping rooms that had her moving furniture around on paper to determine the best use of space without blowing the budget.

Normally, she'd be grumbling about Owen's financial restrictions, but after spending a few days with him, she really wanted to get this right. She'd set up her work space in what would be the managers office. It was one of the spaces that the construction company had finished early on as it would not be part of the TV show. Though it needed carpet, light fixtures and furniture just like the rest of the building, at least it was mostly dust free and she was used to working at a makeshift desk. A couple of saw horses, a thick sheet of plywood, and a comfy chair and she was good to go.

What wasn't so good was Owen. For every few minutes she spent absorbed in her drawings, she spent the same amount of time wondering about the many sides of Owen Farraday. Was it her imagination or with each passing day did the man's smile grow more intense? And those eyes. Deep blue eyes the color of an azure sea were always so full of emotions. Whether it was intense concentration helping out with the construction, the sheer joy playing with his nieces or nephews, or the tenderness dealing with the animals. The man was so much more complex than she'd ever imagined.

A soft knock sounded on the door frame. "Hungry?"

Her gaze shifted to the clock on the wall. The day had really gotten away from her. Not till this second did her stomach rumble to let her know. "Starved."

Owen tipped his head toward the street. "Molly is making her version of sausage and peppers tonight. I haven't tried it yet, but Pax tells me it's one of the best items on the menu."

"Works for me. If I'm going to be securing boards at the blacksmith with the rest of you tonight, I'm going to need fuel."

"If you're tired, we can make do without you."

She shook her head. "Tired, shmired. Good food and good company is all I need. I'll have my second wind in no time."

A lanky fellow whose name she'd forgotten leaned into the doorway. "Hey, sorry to interrupt, Owen, but the film crew wants you back in the lobby. Something needs to be reshot."

"Will do." Owen turned to her. "Sorry. If you want to go ahead to Molly's, I'll catch up with you soon as I can. But I do want to say, for the record, reality TV is most definitely a misnomer. The amount of times that we redo things for the camera is ridiculous."

"If you don't mind, I'd like to watch. Haven't really made time for that yet."

"Sure." He waved her past him and into the lobby.

"There you are." Valerie, Morgan's wife and the producer for the show, came walking across the lobby. In a tight skirt and high heels, she carefully stepped over stray pieces of lumber and miscellaneous power tools. "The guys were showing me some footage they took of the last few minutes of you and Paxton installing the beam to be able to remove that supporting wall and discussing the upcoming Palooza."

Owen nodded.

"We can't be mentioning the Palooza, but there was too much conversation to loop it out. And the beam install is kind of critical so I need you to redo it."

The man's eyes sprang open into huge circles. "You want us to remove and replace the beam?"

"No, no, no." Valerie shook her head. "I want you to go through the last steps when you did all the talking and give me some dialogue I can use."

Owen looked to his brother standing behind Valerie who merely shrugged.

The two got into position under the already installed beam and began chatting about complete and total nonsense. Owen took his hammer and banged the beam into place while Pax pretended to hold it steady. The whole time the two balanced on a ladder, Connie kept holding her breath. Sure enough, the last step off the ladder, Owen's gaze caught hers and he missed the last rung.

Pretty much everyone watching, including her, let out a gasp. She ran up to him, forgetful of the camera crew. "Are you okay?" Her hands immediately went to his ankle that seemed to be twisted underneath him.

"I'm fine." He smiled. "This won't be the first or last rung I've missed."

"Don't forget about the dangling ceiling." Pax didn't look even a little worried about his brother. "This is nothing."

When Owen came to his feet, he did a little jig step. "See. Two perfectly good feet."

Connie blew out a sigh and shook her head. "Sorry. Guess I overreacted."

One of the camera crew walked past them and bent over reaching for a power cord only to bump into Connie's hip, knocking her splat against Owen.

The man wrapped his arm around her waist to steady her, and staring down at her face as she stood plastered against him, he grinned. "Shall we dance?"

Shaking her head, she stepped back. "Not till I've been fed."

When she turned around, Valerie was standing by the camera crew smiling. "Go ahead and at least do a twirl. You know this is the kind of stuff audiences lap up."

Again his eyes widened and then he looked at her, one

questioning brow higher than the other. She had no idea what do so she merely shrugged. Owen gripped her hand in his and twirled her in place.

"Hold on. The camera isn't rolling." Valerie looked to the one guy still operating a camera. When he nodded at her, she nodded at them. "Okay. Now."

Owen twirled her in place once more, and then curling her against him, he did a little Texas Two Step and hummed an old Frank Sinatra tune she couldn't quite pinpoint until he softly sang, "I get a kick out of you."

From the way her cheeks pulled at the corners of her mouth, she knew she was grinning like a fool and didn't care. Who knew a construction project could be so much fun? Or Owen Farraday? Though there was one more thing she'd learned today. Never again would she be able to watch a reality show again without questioning everything she saw. But too bad the filming and the dance had to end. A girl could get used to all this dancing.

"You're bringing kids in here?" Hands on her hips, Connie stood in the open doorway staring into the dilapidated blacksmith shop.

Those exact words were the first thoughts that had come to his mind as well when he set eyes on the place. "Afraid so."

Already, his brothers Quinn and Pax and Ryan were at the far end ripping out old boards, or sanding splinters, or screwing loose boards back in place.

"Are you guys planning on doing any smithing?"

He shook his head. "Nothing with fire this year, but Adam will be playing smithy this time and will shoe some horses. He just won't be making the shoes. The kids should still get a kick out of that."

"I would if I were a kid." Connie dug into her canvass bag and pulled out a thick belt with a couple of leather holsters, then pulling out a hammer, dropped it into one of the loops. "All set."

Owen was pretty sure his jaw momentarily hit the floor when he saw her pulling tools out of that canvas bag that until now had mostly carried her paperwork. "Do you always carry tools around with you like that?"

Hefting one shoulder, she smiled at him. "Had to pick these up from the hardware store this morning. Back home, half my pantry has tools."

"I'm sorry, you keep tools in your pantry?"

Again, she shrugged one shoulder. "Single woman here. I don't need a stocked pantry for what I eat, and I live in an apartment so I don't have a garage. The pantry works for both."

His mind wandered to visions of her pantry, wondering if it was one shelf with a pretty little toolset with a miniature hammer in pink and matching woman-sized tools, or did she really mean that half of the pantry was stocked with more accessories.

"What's that funny look for?"

Now he was the one to shrug one shoulder. "Just trying to picture your pantry."

"Well, it's four foot wide with double bifold doors. On the left side I keep your basic food items: cereals, flours, canned soups, dry goods. On the right, any tools I might need for some project or other. Hammers, nails, screws, saws, chisels, screwdrivers, levels, triangle. You know, the basics."

His mind was scrambling. His interior designer knew about tools. Not what he expected from the woman who always looked like the most strenuous work she did was handling pencils and paper, not hammers and nails.

"Where do you want me to begin?"

He nodded, dragging his thought back to the here and now. "You'll be working with me. In order to not mix old and new wood for now, we are going to take all the boards that have been piled up over here and remove any nails. Pax and Ryan are working on sanding away the big splinters. Normally I wouldn't care about that, but with little kids running around bumping into each other, knocking each other over, or whatever shenanigans they come up with, the last thing I need is to take some kid to the emergency room because he got a splinter up his fingernail, or Lord knows where. Then Neil and Quinn will screw them back in along with the loose boards that are mostly still attached. Aunt Eileen and some others have already cleaned out the decades of debris, so once we're done with the boards, we should be in good shape."

"Sounds good to me."

Boards lined up side by side on a set-up of makeshift sawhorses, Connie had begun working without instruction.

Pulling out several nails with the claw of the hammer, she grunted at one plank and muttered something he couldn't quite understand.

"Need something?"

"Should have brought a cat's paw."

Anyone else and he would have assumed they were talking about felines, but under the circumstances he knew she was talking about a particular tool, one that made pulling nails much easier than with a hammer under certain circumstances. "How do you know about a cat's paw?"

"Not rocket science. Anyone who has worked on a project with one of their six brothers knows what a cat's paw is."

"How many siblings in all do you have?"

"Just the nine of us."

"Nine?"

"Why do you look so surprised, there are six of you. There are seven Farradays here in Tuckers Bluff. What can I say? I come from an Irish Catholic family. Besides, Mom always loved babies. She's still nagging my brothers to get married and give her more grandchildren."

"So none of your brothers are married?"

She shook her head. "Much to my mother's chagrin, only my two sisters are married. At least they gave Mom a few grandchildren so she doesn't drive the rest of us completely nuts wanting more."

"Your family sounds a lot like mine. Except nobody has given my mother grandchildren yet and she makes a point of reminding us about that every opportunity she has."

"At least some of you are getting married now. I'm sure it won't be long before she has a grandchild or two to keep her happy."

The mood his mother was in, he doubted anything would make her happy. Not even when Morgan and Valerie eloped to Oklahoma for a same day wedding, did the woman remain content for more than an afternoon. Instead of focusing on her son's happiness, she sulked over Valerie being from California and Morgan committed to a television show somewhere in Texas. If only he had some idea why his mother disliked West Texas so very much.

"Blasted nail. More stubborn than a determined mule." Flipping the board she was working on over, Connie hammered at the back tip of the nail in an effort to push it through where she could get a good grip on it.

Owen stepped aside and reached for the board. "Sometimes it just takes old fashioned brute force. Let me try." Struggling equally with the hundred or so year old nail, he wielded the full force of the hammer, bringing it down smack dab on his thumb.

Hammer clanking to the floor, Owen let go of a slew of words that would make a sailor blush. Eyes squeezed shut, hand clutched against his chest, maybe it wasn't the kids he had to worry about rushing to the ER.

CHAPTER TEN

How many times had her father warned her to watch her thumbs when using a hammer? Surely if she knew better so did Owen. And yet, the man had successfully smashed his own finger. Gripping his arm, she softly uttered, "Let me take a look, please."

Different brothers called out a chorus of side comments from, *don't mind Mr. Klutz*, to *he has nine more fingers*, to a slightly sarcastic, *just kiss the boo boo and send him back to work.*

"I'll be fine." The way he glared at his brothers, she wasn't sure what hurt him more, his thumb or his pride.

"I'm sure you will, but please let me look anyhow," she insisted.

Nodding his head, she gingerly tugged at the thumb he'd clutched so tightly.

Growing up with brothers, she was pretty good at bumps and bruises, but this one was a doozy. From the way one or two of the brothers winced, they agreed.

"I'll get some ice." Pax turned quickly on his heels.

Owen turned to his brother Neil. "Would you please get the salve out of my tool box?"

"Got it." Like his other brother, Neil took off at a fast clip.

"Can you bend your finger?" she asked.

The man almost stared daggers at her. "It's no big deal."

"Great. Then bend it."

Pressing his lips tightly together, he managed to move the finger a smidge.

"Hurts pretty badly, doesn't it?" Of course it did. What

a dumb thing for her to say.

"Here you go." Pax handed over a blue cotton rag filled with ice.

"I'm going to be as careful as I can, but you didn't break the skin so we have to stop the internal bleeding."

Again, he nodded.

"Where are you in the pecking order?" Owen held onto the rag filled pouch of ice gingerly sandwiched between his and her hands.

"You mean birth order?" She smiled at his choice of words.

Owen nodded. His good thumb slowly rubbing at an exposed portion of skin at the base of her palm.

"I'm the youngest girl. My sisters are first and second, then me, then the six boys. And you?"

"Second to last. Pax is three minutes older than me, and then Neil is the youngest."

She wasn't going to say anything, but the tender way he was drawing soothing circles at the base of her thumb was doing more for her soul than the ice ever could possibly do for his thumb. "If I didn't know better, I would have thought you were the oldest."

"Really?" He smiled. "Why is that?"

Not wanting to say because he was bossy as hell, she merely shrugged a shoulder, then when he winced slightly at the movement her shrugging had caused she flashed him a sorry about that expression.

"Why is that?" he repeated.

"Not going to let me get by with that one, are you?"

He shook his head. "Afraid not."

"Well, you're very particular, confident, good with money. Often character traits of a firstborn."

"I don't suppose confident and particular are synonyms for bossy and demanding?" He bit back a smile so she at least knew he wasn't angry at her.

"Maybe a little."

"I'm not, you know. Bossy and demanding. It's just that I am charged with stewarding our clients' money. I take it seriously."

"Here you go." Neil came hurrying in and handed Connie a small white jar with a green label that had seen better days.

"Thanks." Letting go with one hand, she accepted the jar and turned to him. "I'm going to unscrew this a minute. Keep your hand high – it won't hurt as much if you don't let it go below your heart."

He smiled at her. The man probably knew more about tending to small wounds than she did. After all, it was his salve.

"Need anything else?" Neil asked.

Connie shook her head. "Nope. We're good."

"Then we'll get back to work. Shout out if you need something." All the brothers returned to the opposite side of the large building and resumed their assigned tasks.

"I'll be as gentle as I can. What exactly is this for?"

"This salve will stop me from bruising badly."

"What is it?"

"Don't remember the name, but we used it on the cattle for years before we discovered how well it works on bruising. Mom always just called it cow cream."

That actually made her chuckle.

"No, it's great. Trust me."

For a few seconds, the way his eyes intently locked with hers, she truly believed she could trust this man with anything in the world. "Yes, sir."

"Not sir, just Owen."

"Yes, Owen." She rubbed the salve onto his thumb. "You know, I have a plan."

"Oh," he continued to stare at her fingers rubbing the cream in circular motions, "for what?"

"Those chairs."

His brow buckled in confusion.

"For Chez Gerard. The man was ridiculously annoyed that the chairs we'd picked out were made in China. *Not in my restaurant.* That voice could have been heard all the way in California."

"I know he can be difficult, but the man has a budget, and we need to stick to that."

"Yes. I know that. Which is why I've always had a plan."

Sucking in a deep sigh, he nodded. "Go on."

"The expensive chairs Gerard picked out cost more with the standard fabric. That's the quote you saw."

He nodded again.

"I nixed that and agreed to have just the frame shipped. By upholstering them myself, it's only slightly over budget for the dining area. I managed to convince him that bistro style without the Spanish linen tablecloths would be more in sync with his fresh style of cooking, and his American audience."

The furrow between his brows deepened. "Those tablecloths were a good chunk of the budget."

"I know that too. That's why simple red checkered, made in the USA, cotton cloths were close to offsetting the chairs."

"How close?"

"We're seven hundred and fifty over. I knew with a little effort I could probably shave it down further when I shopped for the accessories."

He bobbed his head. "Why didn't you tell me this sooner?"

"You didn't give me a chance. I came across a few pieces at an estate sale for the bar decorations. They should make a nice difference. Harriet is taking over. You'll probably get the final cost report soon."

The crease in his forehead softened but the harsh edge to his gaze was still intact. If she were a betting woman she'd venture that he was either considering her words or doing math in his head. Whether either of those was a good or bad thing, she didn't have a clue.

Some days Owen could just kick himself. Often he pushed those who worked with him as hard as he pushed his brothers. This was one of those times that he should have simply taken a step back, a deep breath, and given the woman a chance to explain what else she had in mind. He clearly remembered cutting her off more than once, focusing on the quotes he had on paper, and standing firm on the ideology that numbers don't lie. If he were honest with himself, he was mostly annoyed with how she had undermined the rapport he had developed with the restauranteur who now refused to back down from his budget blowing imported chairs that it turns out weren't going to blow the budget after all.

"I'm sorry. I should have listened better."

The way her eyes widened in surprise hit him almost as hard as the realization that he'd been unfair to her. Now it appeared she had no expectations of his being willing to apologize when he was wrong.

"That hard to believe I apologize when I'm wrong?"

She blinked and shook her head. "No. I just didn't expect explaining to be so easy."

Next time he was going to have to remember to hear her out before he jumped to conclusions. He should have realized she'd had a solution. Although she tended to frequently go overbudget on projects, she usually found a way to offset all, if not most of the cost. It was the indigestion in between that drove him nuts. He should know better than to assume because the cost overage was so high, that she would not be able to offset it as she had done so many times in the past. "If I promise to always keep an open mind and not jump to conclusions concerning overages and negative numbers, will you forgive me?"

Her head bobbed like an old bauble doll on the dashboard of a classic car.

Relief washed over him and leaning slightly back, he was actually sorry when she stopped rubbing his bruised thumb and let go.

"Want to try and bend your thumb now?"

He blew out a deep sigh. "Not really, but I will." Holding his hand in front of her face, he waited longer than she liked before finally moving it a fraction of an inch.

"How does that feel?"

He continued to bend it as far as the swelling would allow. "Not great, but I don't think it's broken."

She handed him the salve.

"Thanks. I'll keep rubbing this on every so often for the next twenty-four hours. It'll help with blood clots too."

Her one eyebrow lifted.

"It happens. The blood clots. One particle breaks off and then causes a blockage somewhere important like your heart or lungs."

"Sounds like a smart plan, but I think my contributions for the evening are over."

"Let me help you pack up."

"Nonsense." She shook her head. "You have a bad hand."

"Thumb." It wouldn't be the first or last minor injury he got on a construction site. "And I can still help."

"If you insist." Her tone held more doubt than her words.

He managed to toss her hammer into the satchel, but winced when he reached for her tool belt.

"Better let me do that. I have two good thumbs."

Any other time he would have found her comment curt and reproving, but this time, she had a twinkle in her eye that told him she could tease with the best of them.

She pulled a set of keys out of a side pocket. "I'm all set. I guess I'll see you tomorrow."

"Tomorrow."

She'd slowly turned, called goodbye to his brothers, and walked toward the main street.

"Oh, by the way." He trotted over to her.

"Yes?"

"Tomorrow?" he repeated.

"God willing and if the creek don't rise." Smiling for a long moment, she turned and walked away.

Yep, there was definitely a softer, easygoing side to Miss Connie Swenson. He kept his gaze on her back as she left the building and crossed the street until she was out of sight. Tomorrow couldn't come soon enough.

CHAPTER ELEVEN

Boot heels tapped against the stairs and Connie knew that Meg's husband Adam was coming down to join them before leaving for the office. "Morning."

One of the things Connie loved about staying at the B&B was that morning greeting. Every day, without fail, Adam pulled his wife into a good morning kiss that was just hot enough to make Connie blush, but tame enough for public viewing. She had no idea how two people with life and reality buzzing about them managed to stay so in love.

"Daddy." Their toddling daughter threw her arms around her father's legs and the morning ritual shifted from the wife to the daughter.

The grin on Adam's face and the love sparkling in his eyes for his little girl was enough to keep Connie smiling for the rest of the day.

"I'll be home late tonight." Adam scooped their daughter up into his arms. "The clean up for the Palooza isn't going as smoothly as everyone had hoped. They need extra hands and materials so I'll probably be out at the ranch tonight to help source some wood."

"Wood?" Connie asked. There seemed to be more than enough wood last night.

Adam nodded. "There are a lot of thoroughly rotted boards and panels that can't be salvaged no matter the effort made, so we're going to look for donations before there's a need to cough up more money for a temporary fix."

"Are we talking about the blacksmith building?"

"That and the stables. Owen and Quinn have been trying to find an old wagon coach to give rides in and if they find it, it will have to be housed somewhere designed for that."

Immediately her mind starting turning. Sourcing products is what designers did. And finding ways to squeeze blood from a stone was another skill set that good designers had. Even if that meant free elbow grease on the part of the designer. "Is there enough wood at the ranch?"

"I doubt it. We're not exactly a lumber or salvage yard, but Dad doesn't believe in waste so there has to be some suitable old wood available."

"Got it."

"Okay. I'm out of here." Adam kissed his daughter on the temple, set her down, and gave his wife a more chaste peck on the cheek.

Meg held up the coffee carafe. "Another cup?"

"No, thanks. I've got some phone calls I need to make. Some business to take care of. I'm going to head up to my room for a little bit and head out to the job site later. Maybe after lunch."

Within twenty minutes she was comfortably settled in her room, her laptop in front of her, and the phone number she wanted displayed on the screen. Hopefully, if she could pull off her idea, she might actually be able to be of help to the Palooza after all. Her cell on speaker, the call ringing, she glanced over at the nineteenth century costume hanging on the closet door. The memory of everyone dancing in the Sisters boutique made her smile. So did remembering the sweetness of the moment when she tended to his smashed thumb the night before. All of it making her pray even harder that her idea worked out.

"She's not here. Still."

Owen glanced over his shoulder at his brother Quinn. "Who?"

Rolling his eyes and shaking his head, Quinn turned off the rumbling compressor he'd been using to spray texture in the lobby. "Mother Theresa. Who do you think I mean? The only person who has been using the manager's office. Connie."

For a split second he considered denying that he'd checked the manager's office for the third time this morning in hopes of finding Connie hard at work. "I was just wondering how her plans are coming along."

Shaking his head again, his brother leaned over, turned the noisy contraption back on and muttered over his shoulder, "Sure you were."

Unable to resist his curiosity or concern any longer, he pulled out his cell phone and dialed the B&B.

After the third ring, Meg answered. "Hello."

"Hi there. How's your morning going?"

"Fine. Adam tells me you've run into a snag at the ghost town."

"We'll figure it out."

"If there's one thing I have learned, it's to have faith in a Farraday. Y'all are living examples of *where there's a will there's a way*."

He certainly wasn't going to argue with her on that one. Even his brother Quinn, who had a more gruff disposition that leaned heavily toward the sarcastic, always found a solution to the problem. Whatever the problem was and no matter how much effort or sacrifice the solution required. "No argument from me. Listen, do you know if Connie is in town or is she on her way here?"

"She's up in her room. She said she had some phone calls to do for work. Is something wrong? Do you need me to go get her?"

"No. Nothing important. It can wait."

"All right, then, I'll see you later."

"Will do. And give that sweetheart of yours a kiss from her Uncle Owen."

He could almost hear Meg smiling over the phone. "Deal."

Disconnecting the call, he debated if he should interrupt Connie and call. Not wanting to seem too overbearing, but not wanting her to think he wasn't concerned, he opted for a quick text. *How's your day going?*

Standing silently in the empty office, he stared at his phone, unnecessarily pleased when the message alert sounded.

Great thank you.

Good. I have to do a supply run at the hardware store. Do you have time for lunch?

Sure do.

I'll pick you up at noon. Does that work? He glanced down at this watch and figured that would give him plenty of time to pack up and head back to Tuckers Bluff.

See you then.

Slipping his phone back in his pocket, he quickly thought through what they were working on and what supplies he could pick up from the hardware store that they might actually need.

"There you are." Morgan came into the office. "I've been looking all over for you."

"Sorry. Had a phone call to make and this is the quietest place in the building I could find." It wasn't necessarily the truth of why he was in here, but it wasn't a lie either. The entire hotel was buzzing with construction noise of some sort or other. "What's up?"

"Valerie just ended a teleconference call with the executive producer and some network big wigs."

"And…"

"We don't know."

"I beg your pardon?"

"She said the entire meeting, she had an unsettled feeling in her stomach."

"Maybe it was something she ate."

"Not that kind of unsettled feeling. She's worked with these people long enough that she's pretty sure something's off, but they didn't come right out and say anything. Other than one or two of them is flying out here next week to check on the progress."

Owen didn't like the sound of that at all. "This kind of thing normal?"

"You mean having network executives fly out to a production site out of state? No. That's why Valerie is worried and why I'm giving everyone a heads up. We need to get as much of this done ahead of schedule as we can. Whatever is up, we should cut it off at the pass."

"I think that's a mixed metaphor."

"Whatever." Morgan shook his head and turned toward the door before looking back at his brother. "If I hear anything new from Valerie, I will let you know."

"Fair enough. FYI, I'm running into town. Need anything from the hardware store?"

Morgan shook his head. "No. I'm all set."

Glancing down at his watch, Owen had just enough time to pick Connie up by noon as promised. Making his way through the obstacle course of workers and tools, he tossed his tool belt into the back of his truck and waving at the film crew, pulled out of his parking space and turned the front end toward Tuckers Bluff. Thank heavens he wasn't on the filming schedule for this afternoon.

A couple of phone calls later, including one to his Uncle Sean who was already out in the old barn checking out how much lumber they could spare, and he was pulling up in front of the B&B. Inside, he found Connie at the kitchen island chatting with Meg and playing with Fiona. The little girl seemed totally enthralled with whatever story Connie was sharing with her.

"Hello, ladies."

"Hi." Connie patted the little girl's leg and pushed to her feet. "My purse is by the front door. I'm ready whenever you are."

"Great. How do you feel about corned beef?"

"Love it."

"Then we'll hit the pub for lunch. Jamison is serving corned beef and cabbage tonight and we get the friends and family privilege of having lunch at the pub even though it's not open for business until tonight."

"Sounds good to me."

A wave, a quick goodbye, and a few minutes later they were in front of the old fashioned pub.

"Oh, this is darling." Connie walked in, surveying every nook and cranny of the place.

"Jamie put a lot of heart and soul into the place and honoring our Irish ancestors." He waved to his cousin and escorted Connie to a booth along the far wall. Overhead the soft sounds of yacht rock could be heard.

"Does that have something to do with the odd spelling of Farraday?"

He nodded. "O'Fearadaigh is the original spelling of our family name. Our great-great-grandfather Seamus Xavier O'Fearadaigh came here from county Donegal. From what I understand, like so many other immigrants in those days, when arriving at Ellis Island, the clerk anglicized the spelling of the name. We've been ordinary Farraday ever since."

"It must be fun to know that much about your ancestors. My dad says we've probably been in this country forever and since the family name Swenson is Swedish, he assumes we're of Swedish origins. But for all we know his ancestor had some weird name like Swensonovich or Svenisky, and like your ancestor, the name got changed to something more familiar to the immigration officers and easier to spell."

He chuckled and flipped his hand in a who-knows gesture.

Jamie came walking over with two glasses of water. "No wait staff at this hour so you're going to have to settle for me. You have two choices, corned beef and cabbage, or a Reuben sandwich. What will it be?"

"I'll have my corned beef straight up please." Connie smiled.

His cousin the pub owner chuckled earnestly at her response. "Very good. For that you might get an extra portion."

"Hey, what about me? I like my corned beef straight up with a shot of cabbage too."

Jamie shrugged and grinned at Owen waving a thumb at Connie. "She said it first. I'll be right back."

"I like him." Connie leaned back in the booth. "Actually, I like all your cousins."

"Thankfully, so do I." For a split second his mind wandered to all the fun they'd had as kids visiting the ranch in the summer or during school breaks, what a hole it left in their lives when their mother told them they were no longer welcome.

"Hey, why the glum look? Is it about the wood problem Adam mentioned this morning?"

He shook his head. "Didn't mean to look glum."

At that moment the soft music over shifted to a familiar Glenn Miller tune and Connie's eyes lit up. "Oh boy, I don't hear this very often."

"You like it?"

"I love it. 'In the Mood' is a favorite of mine. Always reminds me of my Uncle Ray."

"Was he a musician or just a music lover?"

"I suppose he was a music lover, but more than that he was a great dancer. Taught me how to do the twist when I was six and the lindy hop when I was twelve. There wasn't a family gathering where the music didn't come on and Uncle Ray would get up to dance."

"Sounds like a fun uncle."

"He was. I loved dancing with him. At my sister's wedding he was ninety-one and danced with every woman in the place, but I was the only one who could lindy with him. My sisters both have two left feet."

"Sounds like Paxton. On the dance floor the poor guy looks like the Tin Man in the *Wizard of Oz* before he was well oiled."

She laughed under her breath. "That bad?"

"Afraid so. Sometimes when he's in rare form other people have to get out of his way for fear of a rogue arm or leg flying in their direction and knocking them out."

"Sounds like my sisters might look like champion dancers compared to him."

"I wouldn't be surprised. I gather your uncle passed away?"

"Years ago. I sure do miss dancing with him. Not a lot of men my age know how to do anything more than sway from side to side. Heck, not a lot of men my parents' age know how to swing dance either. But I digress." She gently slapped her hands palms down on the table. "How is the wood problem coming along?"

"So far, it's not."

"Good."

"Good?" Not at all the response he'd expected—or understood.

"Never mind. What I meant is I think I have a solution."

"I'm all ears." He'd already learned his lesson when it came to Connie and hearing her out. The woman had more business sense than he'd originally given her credit for.

"Do you remember the old Henson farm?"

He had to think about that a minute, before it came to him. "The one on route five that looks to be as old as Oklahoma itself?"

"That's the one. As kids in the summer we would hang out in that dilapidated old barn and tell ghost stories."

"I'm surprised the thing didn't fall down around you." As soon as the last words passed his lips, it struck him what she might be thinking. "I bet that barn is as old as the buildings in Sadieville."

"That's exactly what I was thinking."

"And Mr. Henson probably would be willing to sell some of that wood for a song."

"Actually," she grinned like a cat with a belly full of cream, "less than a song."

"Excuse me?"

"I took the liberty of tracking him down this morning. Just in case."

"And?" He liked where this was going.

"It seems he's getting ready to sell the property and his realtor told him removing the barn would get him a better price. He says if you take the thing down and haul off the wood, you can have it for free."

If he thought he could get away with it, he'd lean over and kiss her. "That's great news." At least it would be if his entire family wasn't here in Texas working. Then again, his father wasn't here. What would be the odds of talking his dad into defying his mother and coming to the land he'd left so long ago?

CHAPTER TWELVE

"Take a deep breath." Eileen straightened in her seat, waved her hand from stomach to chin, and demonstrated taking in a deep inhale and letting it out slowly.

A dutiful niece, Valerie did as her husband's aunt instructed.

"There. Don't you feel better?"

"Not really."

Eileen blew out a sigh.

"Are you two going to play cards or meditate?" Ruth Ann tapped her folded cards on the table.

"You know I don't meditate." Eileen tossed her chip into the center of the table. "I'm in."

Valerie glanced at her cards, shook her head, and tossed a chip in the pot.

"Okay." Sally May added her ante and looking over the rim of her cards, stared at Valerie. "Explain to me again why you're all tied up in knots?"

Carefully pulling two cards from her hand and setting them down on the table, Valerie huffed out a short breath and leaned back in her seat. "In all the years I have been in this business, I have never had a network executive, a sponsor, or a production company hotshot come out where we are filming a series."

"That much I understand," Barbara, another member of the Tuckers Bluff Ladies Afternoon Social Club, set three cards down in front of her. "What I don't understand is why that is such a problem?"

"It's a problem because I cannot think of any good reason for this to happen."

"Well," Sally May folded her cards in front of her, "assuming the worst thing that could happen is the show was canceled, have you ever had a show canceled on you before?"

"There isn't a producer on the planet who has not had a show canceled out from under them at some point in their career. I'm no exception."

"And," Sally May continued, "did they fly to wherever you were filming to fire you?"

"Of course not."

"I see where she's going with this." Ruth Ann shifted her cards around. "If the worst thing that could happen is they cancel the show why would they fly all way out here to tell you that?"

"I have to agree with them, the logic makes sense." Eileen shrugged.

"I know." Valerie bobbed her head. "My mind understands the same logic, but my gut is not agreeing. I just cannot figure out why they're coming."

Barbara shrugged. "So stop trying."

"Easier said than done." Valerie rearranged her cards in her hand.

"When are they coming?"

"They'll be here Wednesday."

"Oh, isn't that when we're doing the dress rehearsal for the Palooza?" Barbara asked.

"This isn't a play. It's not called a dress rehearsal." Sally May shook her head.

Barbara glared at her longtime friend. "So what would you call it?"

"More of a dry run." Sally May shrugged.

"Oh, brother." Valerie squeezed her eyes shut. "I forgot about that. They were already unhappy the Palooza was mentioned in the rushes I sent."

"I'm sure it will be fine." Eileen did her best to bestow that reassuring smile that used to make the kids feel better when something had upended their world.

"I sure hope you're right." Valerie squinted at her cards and fidgeting with her chips, tossed more into the pot. "I'm in for five.”

“Big spender,” Barbara teased.

A chorus of *I'm in* circled the table.

“Read 'em and weep.” Valerie laid out a full house aces high.

“See?” Eileen tossed her cards into the pile. “Things are looking up already.”

“And… cut.” The director gave the crew a thumbs up. “As usual, well done. I think this is going to be almost as startling a renovation as the homestead.”

Owen had to admit, the hotel was coming together beautifully. The addition of the penthouse was actually ahead of schedule. Framed up in less than a week, the plumbing lines had been run, and the composition roofing was going on today.

“Have you heard back from Dad?” Brushing construction dust from his hands, Paxton came to a stop at his brother's side.

“A little while ago.” After talking with Mr. Henson about reclaiming the barn wood, Owen had to take a night to think through his options, and then when he was sure that having his dad drive the trailer filled with wood to Texas is truly the easiest solution, and the most cost-effective, he sat down with his brothers to get their thoughts. In the end everyone agreed it was worth a shot so Owen called his father and pitched the situation.

“The crazy thing is,” Paxton shook his head, “this shouldn't be so difficult. Family should be able to come and go without drama.”

“No, it shouldn't. On the bright side, once Dad heard this was all about underprivileged and foster kids, he was on board. He's over there now getting started. As available, other crew teams are going to help.”

“That's a big project for Dad to be starting alone.”

“Thankfully there's not much of that old barn left. Dad

can put a good dent in the project."

"I know I'm going to regret this, but what about Mom?"

Every time Owen's phone rang or a text dinged, he expected to hear his mother barking on the other end. It was bad enough to have her calling constantly, prodding all his siblings to hurry up and come home, to take more local projects, to call her more often. The fact that they worked an eight hour day didn't seem to slow her expectations. When Morgan and Valerie married and she found out that thanks to both their jobs, they would be in Texas more than Oklahoma, that gave her more reasons to blow up their phones. The real kicker was when Neil told their mom and dad his intentions to propose to Nora. Not that proposing was a problem, it was her being from Texas with no intention of moving to Oklahoma that had their mother crying buckets of tears over losing her son. There was no calming her and then Neil let it slip that Nora lived in Tuckers Bluff and all hell broke lose. His mother had texted or called him so often he couldn't focus on work.

Now that his father had informed him he would make the long drive to deliver the trailer, Owen kept expecting his mother to light up his phone again.

"So far I haven't heard a word from her. I don't know if Dad has told her yet, or if he's simply not telling her where he's taking the wood."

Paxton nodded. "Does Uncle Sean know Dad's coming?"

"Not yet. But he's always said Mom and Dad are welcome any time, so hopefully it won't be a problem."

"Aunt Eileen will probably be over the moon."

"That she will." His aunt and his mother were polar opposites when it came to corralling their brood. Aunt Eileen did it with good food, lots of love, and southern power of persuasion. His mother, on the other hand, had never learned the old adage that you got more with sugar than vinegar.

"I'm going to see how things are going downstairs."

Paxton rolled his eyes and grinned knowingly at his brother. "Yes, why don't you do that. Find something downstairs to check on."

Since it was almost quitting time, and they couldn't do anymore work on the stable or smithy shop until the reclaimed wood arrived, he hoped he could talk Connie into joining him for dinner and a little surprise. The least he could do to thank her for saving the day. It still surprised him to think that his always over budget designer was the one who came up with a super budget friendly solution. The woman was amazing.

Hurrying down the last few steps, he was lost in thought considering his surprise for her when the sound of giggles caught his attention. He expected to find Connie in the manager's office, but he hadn't expected to hear multiple women's voices. Slowly approaching the office, he nudged the ajar door fully open. Blinking he looked from one chair to another. *What the heck*?

"For expensive cotton, this one's pretty scratchy." Molly, the food truck cook, whipped the sheet off her bare shoulders and tossed it onto a pile on the floor.

"This is why we had to do this. Can you imagine sleeping on that?"

Molly cringed just as Connie heard a man clearing his throat.

"Is this not a good time?"

Catherine Farraday chuckled. "Take off your shirt and join the fun."

If only Connie had her phone handy to take a photo of the wide eyed shock on Owen's face. "We're sheet testing."

"I see," he said slowly.

Years of working with commercial design had taught her to expect the unexpected. The last thing she needed was to spend a small fortune stocking sheets that weren't going to be up to the standards of the new luxury ghost town hotel.

Rather than spend all day or more testing the sheets on

her own, Connie had corralled a few other women to help. Not that men couldn't have helped, but women tended to be more sensitive to the different sensations stirred by fabric. So supplying old-fashioned peasant blouses to expose everyone's shoulders, the women had spent the last hour rubbing sheet after sheet across their backs and shoulders as if towel drying their skin.

A loud sneeze snapped everyone's attention away from the tall, good-looking construction cowboy in the doorway. They all turned to see Molly sneeze again, then using her right hand, scratched her left shoulder.

"You all right?" Connie asked.

Molly shook her head. "It's my allergies."

"What are you allergic to?" Catherine asked.

"Well..." She sneezed once, twice, three times before rubbing her eye and shaking her head at Connie. "These are one hundred percent cotton?"

Connie nodded. "That's what the labels say: one hundred percent Egyptian cotton."

"'Fraid not. This sucker has rayon in it."

"How do you know?" Owen asked.

Molly sneezed again and pushed to her feet. "I'm all...*sneeze*...allergic to...*sneeze*...rayon."

"You better go home and take a shower or something." Catherine stood next to her hovering.

"I have allergy meds in my truck. I'll just pop over, take a couple of pills, and take a minute to wipe my shoulders clean. I should be right... *sneeze*...as rain before the dinner...*sneeze*...crowd."

Catherine reached for a blouse draped over the back of a chair and slipping her arms through it, put the shirt on over the peasant blouse. "I'd better get back to the ranch before Connor thinks I ran off with the milkman."

"Ha," Connie barked. "Like that will ever happen."

Molly beat Catherine out the door, Catherine waved at Connie and paused a moment in the doorway to give her cousin-in-law a peck on the cheek.

"Need help with anything?" Owen's request was guarded. It was obvious to any idiot that he was still baffled by what he'd just seen.

Connie slipped a button down shirt on over the peasant blouse. "Not really. But your frugal self will appreciate the money I'm saving the budget. The sheets that Molly determined were not 100% cotton were the most expensive choice among all the sheets."

"I may succeed in making a penny pincher out of you yet." Owen smiled.

"I've always loved the art of the deal. But sometimes I don't have a choice and we simply have to go the more costly route to achieve our final goal in the end."

"Understood."

"Good. So what brings you to my temporary office?"

"I wanted to thank you for your help with the wood issue. I'm hoping you're free for dinner tonight?"

"You don't have to do anything to thank me, but that said, I have no plans." She smiled, doing her best to hide just how pleased she was.

"Good, then I'll follow you back to town to leave your car and we'll go from there."

"Actually," she pulled her handbag out of the desk drawer, "I rode in with the Sisters this morning. They planned to be here all day restocking the mercantile and freshening things up for Monday's dry run."

"Even better. We'll get a head start on dinner."

She glanced down at her watch. Only four thirty. "Uh, isn't it a little early still?"

"Not if we're having dinner in Butler Springs."

"Oh." She hadn't expected that. "We could do the pub for dinner. If the corned beef was any indicator, I bet the food will be delicious."

"It would, but I have a surprise in mind."

"Really?" She flung the bag over her shoulder. "Care to give a little hint?"

"Not really. But I hope you'll be pleased." His grin was wide, and sparkling, and reminded her of a little kid who had pulled off a trick on his little brother. She just hoped when all was said and done, she was as happy as him and not unsettled like a kid brother who'd been bested.

CHAPTER THIRTEEN

One of these days, Owen was going to buy a real car. Before he even asked Connie to join him for dinner, he'd cleaned out the inside of his work truck. The only time he ever took a rag and cleaner to his vehicles was when he had a date, and lately, that wasn't very often. A second comfortable car would make so much more sense. At least he had a step up to make climbing in easier.

Taking hold of the grab bar, Connie stepped up and into the cab and lips pressed tightly closed, scanned her surroundings, nodding. "Nice job."

"Thanks." He closed the door and circled the hood.

"For a second, I thought I was in the wrong car."

He shrugged. "Every so often things have to be organized."

"Right." She smiled. "Organized. So, where are we going?"

"That depends. Do you prefer steak, Italian, or seafood?"

"I don't suppose all of it is the answer you're looking for?"

"Actually," he smiled at her, "that's exactly what I wanted to hear, because I made a reservation at the best steakhouse in town."

"Okay, now I'm hungry. I love a good rib eye."

"Then you're in for a treat. This is West Texas cattle country and no one can grill a steak like the Ranch To Table restaurant. But just in case, they have seafood too. I recommend the crab cakes. How do you feel about Key Lime pie?"

"Love it."

"Then save a little room."

"Don't have to tell me twice. I've been known to have dessert first just to make sure I don't miss out."

A deep belly laugh slipped out. "I love it. I'm going to have to try that."

"I will if you will?" She grinned at him with a high wattage smile that made her eyes sparkle with delight.

"Deal."

"So tell me." Tugging at her seat belt, Connie shifted in her seat to better face him. "Were you always good at math and numbers?"

He shook his head. "Hated math in grade school. I wanted to be a rodeo star and as long as I could count seconds on a bronc, and my winnings of course, who needed math."

A sly grin took over her face. "I bet you would have made a great rodeo champ."

"Maybe." He shrugged. "Though I'm much less likely to break every bone in my body with the job I have."

She chuckled. "Unless you fall through the ceiling."

"You too? It's bad enough my brothers feel obliged to bring that up every so often."

"Brothers like to tease each other. Especially if you're the younger one."

"They say they're just doing their part to keep me humble."

"Well, there's that too." Her smile turned more wistful. "So what changed?"

"Changed what?"

"The dream, and the math. Because you're not going to make me believe you're not good at math. No one can make a company like the Farraday Brothers Construction as successful as you have being bad at numbers."

If he'd learned anything in his lifetime, it was that the old cliché *life is what happens while you're busy making other plans* was totally true. "I was around eleven when everything that could go wrong with a cattle operation did. From losing a slew of cattle when the drinking pond got contaminated with run off from a nearby development, to a fire taking out the stash of winter hay, and a few other variables in between, the family ranch took a nasty hit. At first Dad pretended it was not the end of the world that all would be well again, but I saw the toll it took on him. We started working together more. He taught me how to do the books, and I started finding places where we could cut back. Dad sold a small lot of land to those same developers to help get us through, but it was tough. Two years later, we were back on our feet and I'd learned that given the chance I actually liked working with numbers. Not enough to become an accountant, but enough to tinker with deal making."

"Dreams of rodeo buckles fell by the wayside and real estate mogul took its place."

"I wouldn't go that far, but yeah, as we each started taking up a hammer and nails to help hold the old ranch together, we discovered we liked that better than mucking stalls or chasing down lost calves. Mixing construction skills with real estate seemed like a no brainer." He tipped his head to get a better look at her. "What about you? Have any childhood dreams?"

She let out a low chuckle. "Lots of them. Let's see. At four I wanted to be an opera singer, at six a ballerina, at eight a princess—"

"Lofty ambitions." He smiled at her.

"Oh, but I smartened up. By ten I realized money made things happen and waiting around for a rich prince to make me a princess wasn't very practical."

As she explained redirecting her ambitions to doctor, or lawyer, he pulled into the restaurant parking lot.

When he opened her car door for her, she slid one leg out in front of her and paused to study the building. "Oh, this looks really nice."

"It's even better inside." Extending his hand to help her out, he held on a little longer than he probably should have before letting his hand shift to the small of her back and guiding her up the walkway.

The maitre'd led them to a small table by a large window overlooking a beautifully landscaped patio. The place always reminded him of cities like New Orleans or Savannah with their brick patios and tons of greenery. He beat out the man to pull out Connie's chair. When she was all settled in, he leaned forward. "What dream finally won?"

"In college I realized I was not cut out to be a doctor or a lawyer. Mostly because I hated organic chemistry and the thought of more years of education before I could begin to earn a living left me dizzy. So I took my degree in business management and went to work for Harriet as her office manager."

"From office manager to interior designer extraordinaire."

"Thank you."

"You're welcome, but it's true. You're very good. Even if you did test my nerves with some of your expenditures."

"Sorry about that, but I do fix it in the end."

"You do, but the trip can be rough."

She tipped her head and hefted a shoulder in a sassy gesture. "It's what makes life interesting."

"Does this mean that you're living your dreams?"

"Almost. I want to have my own firm, take the clients I want, and work on the projects that mean something to me. Don't get me wrong. I really love my job, but I don't want to work for someone else forever."

He could understand that. He just had to ask himself, if she had her own firm, would she still want him for a client?

Connie couldn't believe she was sitting here at a fancy restaurant with the most amazing food in front of her, telling Owen all her hopes and dreams. They had indeed eaten dessert first. Though they ordered one slice of pie with two forks, and somewhere along the way they went from nibbling on the confection to having a fork war. She felt like a happy kid without a care in the world.

One good flick of her wrist and she sent Owen's fork flying. Immediately her hand flew to her mouth. "Oops. Sorry."

Thankfully he just laughed. He had a great laugh. How had they worked together all these years and all she had ever seen was his stern pencil pushing demeanor?

He waved a finger at her. "After dinner we're having a rematch."

"You're on."

The waiter brought their food and when Connie cut into the steak and took her first bite she almost moaned with delight. "Now this is the stuff dreams are made of."

"Normally we're supposed to under promise and over deliver, but this place can hold its own."

Setting her fork on the plate, she swallowed her bite and studied Owen. "That says an awful lot about you."

"What, that I like steak?"

"No. Under promise and over deliver. That's what you do with your budgets. Why you get so bent out of shape when I go over budget." She actually felt that after tonight, she understood Owen even better.

As soon as Owen had paid the bill, he pushed to his feet and extended his hand. "Ready for your surprise?"

"Absolutely." It was all she could do to stop herself from squealing with delight. "Did I ever mention I love surprises?"

He shook his head. "I'll keep that in mind. I just hope I haven't over promised."

"I doubt that seriously." She watched the side of the road as Owen pulled out of the parking lot and turned down the city streets as if he'd been roaming this town his whole life. With every turn the excitement churning inside her spread like wildfire.

"And here we are." He turned into a parking lot and pulled up to the valet. Before she could react, the young man had her door open while another kid who barely looked old enough to drive, took Owen's keys in exchange for a claim ticket.

Standing in front of the building, she looked at the large sign with red letters in cursive spelling *Red Jacket*.

"Come on." He nudged her along, watching her closely.

Not till she got to the door did she notice the other

etching on the glass front. *Dance club*. Confusion was quickly replacing the excitement that had been licking at her insides.

In the door, he paid the cover charge and then slipped the man directing patrons a tip and was led directly to a round table at the front edge of the large wooden dance floor.

So focused on her surroundings and wondering what exactly was her surprise going to be, she hadn't paid any attention to the music overhead until Owen stretched his hand out to her. "Shall we?"

As if suddenly given a pair of eyeglasses, everything came clearly into view. The people moving about the dance floor, not in a two step, or the boring can't dance sway, they were spinning and turning and moving about like characters from a mid last century musical. They were in a swing club.

"I know I'm not your Uncle Ray, but I have been known to cut a mean rug."

Connie loved that he was trying to give her something she missed badly, but the bigger surprise was when they stepped onto the floor and he took hold of her hand. The moment he pulled her into a standard hold for swing dancing, she knew this man had done this before.

At that very moment, Glenn Miller's "In the Mood" started playing and she realized the tip wasn't for the table but the song. Five short minutes later, she'd been twirled, spun, dipped, and bounced and couldn't remember ever having had a better time. At least not since Uncle Ray stopped dancing.

The Glenn Miller tune faded and another quick paced rhythm took its place, and she was thrilled when rather than retake their seats, Owen twirled her out and in for another go at the new song.

She'd lost track of how many songs they'd danced to when Owen twirled her into his side, the song faded, and dipping his chin, he dared to do what she'd been waiting for all week. The kiss was soft, and sweet, and ended all too quickly.

Another song came on, and still holding her tightly

against him, he kept his gaze linked with hers. "Another song, or time for a break?"

Too bad the options didn't include time for another kiss. Like everything else about this part of Texas, kissing Owen was most definitely something she wouldn't mind getting used to.

CHAPTER FOURTEEN

This project seemed to have flown by. Or maybe it was the company Owen had been keeping. The old adage *time flies when you're having fun* seemed to be perfectly apropos. There were so many things he'd come to learn about Connie that had surprised and delighted him. Now that their work was almost done, he needed to figure out his next move. Of course, his first instinct was to pull her into his arms and kiss her for real. Not just the short, sweet peck on the lips that had stayed on his mind ever since the other evening, but a long, deep kiss that could tell her everything he was feeling.

"Since when are you part of the clean up crew?" Morgan came down the gleaming wooden steps.

Gripping the mop handle, Owen lifted his attention from the floor to his older brother. "Since no one else can get here in time to fix things up before the Palooza this weekend."

His oldest brother nodded. "Got another one?"

"Nope. But there are plenty of rags in a box on the check-in desk. Help yourself and wipe anything covered in a layer of dust.

"Oh, dear heavens. They're almost here." Valerie burst through the freshly stained double doors. "Why is everything still so dusty?"

"Because we just finished up down here…" Owen flipped his wrist and looked at his watch. "An hour ago."

"What about the rooms upstairs?" Valerie's gaze lifted to the second floor no one could see.

Morgan walked up to her, and rubbing a soothing hand down her arm, kissed her soundly on the lips. "Connie is putting on the final touches. Everything will be camera ready for the last shoot soon."

His poor sister-in-law was totally flustered. A few days ago she'd received notice that the sponsor and his wife would be arriving a couple of days later than planned, which put them in Sadieville right in the middle of the Palooza. Since she knew the networks didn't want any mention of the Palooza in the reels, having them here at the same time only added to Valerie's jitters.

"There are two long black limousines kicking up a lot of dust down the road." Neil came in the front door. "Should we let the welcoming committee meet them or cut them off at the pass?"

"Welcoming committee?" Valerie spun around to face her husband.

"I think he means the Sisters." Owen tried not to laugh at the stricken look on his sister-in-law's face. "They've been talking about nothing but showing off the town to the sponsors ever since they heard they were coming to Sadieville."

"Oh, boy." Valerie spun back around to face the double doors. "How nervous must I be if I have no idea if that's a good or bad thing?"

Morgan chuckled softly, pulled his wife into a soothing hug. "Would Aunt Eileen be better?"

Valerie's head snapped up from its place on his shoulder. "Is she here too?"

"That would be an affirmative." Morgan gave a curt nod.

"Oh, boy." Valerie pulled away, looked to her husband and brothers-in-law, and blew out a deep sigh. "They're going to have to meet them sooner or later. And whatever they're here for, I doubt anything the ladies do or say is going to change their mind."

"That's my girl." Morgan kissed her on the forehead and Owen felt a twinge of envy course through him.

Two of his brothers had found the loves of their lives and now that Owen had found the woman he could love for the rest of his life, he wished he had the liberty to hold and comfort Connie at will. *The rest of his life.* Like grabbing a live wire, it suddenly hit him with shocking clarity that Connie was the only woman for him.

"You okay, bro?" Paxton came out of the manager's office and slapped his brother on the back. "You look like you swallowed a fishing hook."

Owen blinked at his identical twin and shook his thoughts away. "Fine. Just running through last minute things in my mind." Like how to convince Connie that he was the only guy for her.

"The dry run for the Palooza was a smashing success. I'm sure you've got this." Pax took a step back. "I'm popping over to the stables to see if Dad and Uncle Sean need any help."

"How's that going?" Valerie asked.

"I think fine. When Dad pulled onto the ranch I thought Uncle Sean was going to cry. Neither said a word for a long awkward minute and then they fell into a warm embrace and I wondered if they were ever going to let go."

"The really weird thing about it," Neil interjected, "is that they haven't said a word about our staying away or what went down. They're acting as if nothing ever changed and they've always been together."

"I suppose that could be a good thing." Valerie shrugged.

"Maybe," Owen mumbled. And then again, like a long slow burning fuse on dynamite, maybe not.

Rumors ran through this production site faster than a white water rapids on a rainy day. Connie had fluffed the last pillow and straightened one more wall print when Owen texted her that the sponsors would be here any minute. Her foot had barely hit the last step of the newly refinished staircase when Valerie practically squealed, "They're here."

As nervous as Valerie seemed to be wondering what could bring the biggest sponsor of the show to West Texas,

Connie was equally curious. Not about why they were here, but what were sponsors like. What must it be like to decide if TV shows live or die. So to speak.

"I think I should probably go see what Paxton needs. I don't think the new guests need to have a reception committee." For about a second Connie thought Owen was going to lean in and kiss her. Ever since that one and only sweet, toe curling kiss, every time he came close enough for her to smell his cologne, goose flesh spread up her arms in hopeful anticipation of another kiss. Oh, well. As Scarlett O'Hara once said: Tomorrow is another day.

No sooner had the side door shut behind him, when the long black limousine pulled up and the back door opened. One dangling foot appeared, and all Connie could see was the red bottomed sole. Of course somebody this important could afford to spend a thousand dollars for a pair of designer shoes. It took another long minute for the other foot to appear, and finally a tall slender woman came to stand taking in the exterior of the building. Not a thing about the woman was what Connie had expected. Not that she had any idea what famous Hollywood executives should look like, but a woman in her mid-40s wearing bright pink leggings with a matching pink leopard print top exposing one shoulder, along with large hoop earrings and sunglasses as big as her face was not even close to Connie's expectations.

Circling around from the other side of the vehicle, a man came to stand beside the bleached blonde. In neatly pressed slacks, with an equally starched button down short sleeve shirt and matching brown leather belt and shoes, the guy dripped of old money. There wasn't a doubt in Connie's mind that the man's shoes cost as much as his companion's, maybe even more. He also had a few years on the woman. Okay, maybe more than a few. If she were to make a guess, she'd put her money on the feline wannabe had been the man's midlife crisis twenty years ago.

"Mrs. Neuman. What a pleasure to see you again." Valerie smiled at the woman.

"I can't believe I'm here." The lady clapped her hands

and walked into the lobby, her gaze falling on the light tan leather sofas that had been placed throughout the large space. Her brows dipped, but no wrinkles appeared. Apparently besides dressing like a color blind college student on spring break, she obviously had an up close and personal relationship with a dermatologist in an effort to stay young. Connie hated to tell her it wasn't working.

The lady spun around to face the few people in the lobby. One by one they were all introduced, and expected pleasantries exchanged when the blonde focused on Valerie. "Have you seen many ghosts yet?"

"I'm sorry." Valerie blinked. "What was that?"

"Ghosts. It's a ghost town. I read Joanna Farraday's book on this and other Texas ghost towns. There has to be ghosts."

"Oh. Well, that's just a reference to the abandoned state the town used to be in. We don't have any ghosts."

Mrs. Neuman waved her off. "Nonsense. I heard about the woman crying for help in the middle of the night."

"Those were just peacocks," Neil offered. "It was a bit of a surprise, but peacocks squawking sound very much like a person calling for help."

The lady shook her head at him. "What about all the moving objects? The poor cameraman was so spooked he won't work on the project anymore."

This time Morgan stepped in. "Rest assured you do not have to worry about ghosts. There's nothing to be afraid of. The town is perfectly normal. The moving furniture had nothing to do with spirits."

"I'm not afraid." The lady was practically shuddering with excitement. "Why do you think I'm here? I want to meet the ghosts!"

Connie didn't know whose jaw dropped the farthest. Neil looked to Morgan, Morgan look to Valerie, Valerie looked to Connie, and Connie just shrugged.

"I'm afraid we don't have ghosts." Valerie flashed a weak smile.

"I'm not surprised." Again, the lady shook her head and slowly turned about taking in the lobby. "This is all wrong.

Why would Miss Sadie want to visit this place? It's too," she looked at the sofa then up at Valerie, "too contemporary."

It was Connie's turn to speak up. "We were going for a traditional look that would allow for comfort but still blend in with the mood of the previous centuries. It's very inviting."

"That won't do at all." Mrs. Neuman's arms waved about. "If you want Miss Sadie to visit our guests, she has to feel welcome. All of this has to go. We need to bring in some brothel bling."

Connie knew her eyes had to be bugging out. What the heck was brothel bling?

"You need color, and texture, and pizzazz." The sponsor's wife shook her head, once again scanning the lobby. "Pink. We need lots of pink. And velvet. Madams love velvet. Ooh and crystals. You know, I'm a bit psychic myself and crystals really do help communicate with the beyond."

From what Connie could see, the woman was more psycho than psychic. But what was more worrisome was the sponsor standing beside his wife nodding. Surely he didn't agree with her? "There are already plans in the works for the grand opening and changing up the décor now will cost more than the sponsors want to pay." She turned to the husband. "Isn't that correct?"

"It's a consideration." The man's response wasn't the strong endorsement she'd been hoping for.

"Hello." Aunt Eileen came into the lobby, and dressed in full costume, walked up to the lady demanding pink. "I'm Eileen Farraday. Nice to meet you."

Rather than accept the proffered hand, the blonde poked Aunt Eileen in the ribs. "Oh, you're real."

"Excuse me?"

"I thought you might be a ghost."

"I see." Eileen glanced sideways at her nephews. "I guess I should have worn more make up today."

That attempt at humor had most people chuckling and the blonde carrying on about how we all needed to make the ghosts feel more welcome. For the first time since Valerie went into near panic mode at the anticipated arrival of the company rep footing a good chunk of the money for this renovation, Connie was about to start panicking herself. Owen was the company face, he should be here to talk some sense into the woman. Or Paxton, he had a way with the ladies. Someone was going to need to reel this woman in, and fast. But one thing was sure, over her dead body would a single stitch of brothel bling cross that threshold.

"Exactly how much power does this man and his plastic-coated wife have?" Aunt Eileen set a bowl of mashed potatoes on the dining room table.

Valerie placed a basket of bread beside the potatoes and took a seat. "Too much. If he wants to pull the plug, the show can get cancelled and the funds for the renovations will evaporate."

"I don't care if the show is cancelled, but the costs of completing the plans for the town are something Tuckers Bluff is not capable of handling on their own." Owen didn't need to be a whiz at numbers or math to figure that one out. The costs of converting the antiquated hotel into a luxury boutique destination for the wealthiest tourists was not a pittance. The sponsorship and television show was the only way the town could maintain control of the different businesses, not to mention reap the benefits of the profits— once they started rolling in.

"So what are we going to do?" Morgan grabbed hold of his wife's hand and gave her a reassuring squeeze. "Somehow we have to convince Marla Neuman and her husband that ghosts are not the way to bring in tourists."

"Actually," Uncle Sean reached for the platter of steamed asparagus, "a little ghostly interaction does attract a goodly number of tourists. I just read an article on a haunted castle in Scotland. People pay good money to fly to Scotland and sleep with the ghosts."

Valerie stared at her uncle-in-law. "I don't think that decorating the hotel in pink velvet is going to bring tourists or ghosts."

"I'm onboard with that." Connie poked at a piece of meat and slid the morsel into her mouth.

Uncle Sean laughed. "I agree—pink velvet doesn't work. I'm simply saying, don't discard the appeal a little minor ghostly activity can have on the tourist trade."

"All I know," Aunt Eileen stabbed at a pork chop, "is if that woman spends all day tomorrow at the Palooza poking people in costume to see if they're ghosts, we're going to have some very bruised residents."

"Which brings us back to, what are we going to do?" Paxton dangled his fork in the air. "Because it sounds like telling her to go to Hades isn't on the table."

"I'll work on Mr. Neuman. When he's not around his wife, he's actually a very reasonable man." Valerie used her fork to push her food around while she considered her words. "I could probably use Owen's skill at numbers to show him that brothel bling isn't as profitable as casual elegance."

"I'm sorry," Uncle Sean paused to face Valerie, "did you say brothel bling? What the heck is that?"

"The pink, pink, and more pink," Connie clarified.

"Owen and I can give a shot to enlightening Mr. Neuman on the bare bone realities of the time line and budget constraints," Valerie continued, "but it's going to be up to the rest of you men to somehow convince Mrs. Neuman that the project will be better without making changes."

If Mr. Neuman was the numbers man that Morgan expected him to be, it wouldn't be hard to show him that making any dramatic changes at this stage of the game would only succeed in putting the project deep in red ink.

"Why us?" Paxton asked.

Water glass in hand, Valerie looked at him over the rim. "Let's just say Mrs. Neuman appreciates a good looking member of the male population. And all of you definitely fit the bill."

"Besides," Connie smiled at the man, "there isn't a woman in Oklahoma who wouldn't sell her mother for a little attention from the fun-loving Paxton Farraday."

That had Owen's head snapping up. Had she been one of every woman in Oklahoma?

"Valerie is right." Connie waved a hand at Paxton. "A little charm can go a long way in a mess like this.

Paxton shook his head. "I don't know what difference it's going to make, but if you think charming the lady will change her mind about trying to reach Miss Sadie, I'll give it the college try."

"Fair enough." Valerie nodded. "But whatever you do, don't tick her off."

"Got it." Paxton sighed. "Be kind, polite, anti pink, and under no circumstances upset Mrs. Neuman. No promises."

The other men around the table nodded in agreement. Owen wasn't all so sure that Mrs. Neuman would be convinced otherwise, but he was willing to make the effort. After all, something had to work out.

CHAPTER FIFTEEN

"**D**oesn't everyone look lovely." Sissy stood in the middle of the mercantile. People were gathering in groups all over to prepare for the start of the Palooza and Connie was thrilled to have been included with the Farraday women. She and Meg and the other wives who lived in town dressed at the B&B, then they made their way to the ranch to meet up with the remaining Farraday women. The men had left at the crack of dawn for Sadieville to make sure there was nothing overlooked before the buses of kids began arriving.

Connie had no idea who was more excited, the women, the men, or the kids they were expecting shortly. She and the other ladies had been setting up the gifts Owen had ordered for the kids. Piles and piles of bonnets for the girls and cowboy hats for the boys. And just in case some of the girls preferred to be cowgirls, there were extra hats for them as well. It still boggled her mind that Mr. Penny Pincher and always on budget was actually extremely generous.

"How are you holding up?" Aunt Eileen fluffed a fancy wide brim hat that a woman of means might have worn over a hundred years ago.

"Fine."

Still holding the hat in her hand, Aunt Eileen dipped her chin and stared up at Connie. "So the crazy woman has seen the light?"

Okay, maybe not that fine. "She wants to do a séance."

"Séance?"

"That's right. She thinks the Parlor House is the perfect spot and even has the Sisters agreeing. Something about getting Sadie's ghost to explain to me that my designs are all wrong for the hotel."

"I see." Aunt Eileen put the hat on the mannequin and turned around to face her again. "For today, I suggest we all focus on the kids. The self appointed ghostbuster will just have to wait."

Oh, how Connie hoped it would be that simple. Mrs. Neuman had gone into the mercantile late yesterday and bought a saloon girl costume. No doubt hoping to appeal to Miss Sadie. "If only Sadie would appear and tell the woman to leave me the heck alone."

Eileen stared at her for a second before the corners of her lips tipped upward in a sly grin. "Yes, wouldn't that be nice."

"Yes, it would." Considering how much trouble this one woman was creating for such a well oiled machine, it suddenly struck Connie that maybe they could persuade Mrs. Neuman to see the light. "I don't suppose you know anything about séances?"

"Me? Heck no."

"What about staging a séance?"

"Now why would I want…" Eileen Farraday broke into a huge smile. "Smart lady. Let me see if I can get a few people on board. We might be able to make your wish come true."

"What are you thinking?" They didn't have much time.

"Not sure. You just need to come to the séance. If I can't get the Ghost of Bordellos Past to appear, we'll have to go to plan B."

Connie nodded. "And what's plan B?" That was a foolish question since she had no idea what plan A was.

"Haven't thought of it yet. I need to go see a man about a horse." Eileen hurried toward the front door.

"I think I'll go see who else needs any help," she called after the matriarch. Her instinct was to follow the woman, but from the stories she'd heard Owen and the others tell, she was probably better off letting Eileen figure this out on her own.

"You do that, dear." Eileen's smile widened as she waved and practically marched up the street.

Connie had barely made it halfway up the wooded sidewalk when she bumped smack into none other than Marla Neuman. "Why, don't you look just adorable in that dress."

Somehow, what should have been a compliment sounded like anything but. "Thank you, Mrs. Neuman. You look well in that dress also."

"I do, don't I?" She flicked at the dress, adjusting her ample cleavage, no doubt bought and paid for like the plastic smile, and leveled her gaze with Connie. "My husband told me to look for Mr. Farraday about the hotel. You wouldn't know where I could find him."

"Did he say which Mr. Farraday?"

The lady leaned back, her eyes wide, and her lips slightly parted in surprise. "How many are there?"

For a second Connie began to count how many were expected today and instead settled for, "More than one. Any clue which one he wants you to see?"

"The one who handles the money."

At that moment, Paxton came strolling down the middle of the street, his spurs banging on the dusty road.

"Isn't that just like a Farraday to appear when you need them?" Connie figured Paxton would be better at escorting the woman to find Owen. After all, they had agreed last night that if anyone could charm her into changing her mind, it would be him.

"He's Mr. Farraday?"

"One of them."

"Oh my." The woman fanned her hand under her chin, tugged the already low cut neckline even lower. "This could prove to be the most fun I've had with numbers in a very long time."

"Oh, no. He's not—"

"Shh. Here he comes." The woman's gaze remained fixed on Paxton strutting the rest of the short distance between them.

On second thought, Connie noticed how Marla Neuman was practically drooling at Paxton. If she wanted Owen, what harm would it do to let her believe Paxton was Owen?

As long as Paxton didn't have to talk money, all would be fine. Besides, she doubted that woman ever discussed money, only spent it.

"Hello, ladies." Like a true gentleman of the old west, Paxton tipped his hat. "Welcome Mrs. Neuman."

"Please call me Marla."

He nodded. "I'm told you were interested in a full tour of what we've been doing to this forgotten town."

"Oh, yes. I'm dying to see more."

Connie had no idea a woman could bat her eyes so quickly.

Extending his elbow to her, Marla latched onto him and flashed a wide smile. "I especially don't want to miss the Parlor House."

"Absolutely." Spinning the two of them around to return up the street, Paxton winked at Connie and urged Marla forward.

Usually Connie wasn't a person who believed in premonitions, but right about now, she had a gut feeling today was not going to go as planned. The question was, would that be a good or bad thing?

"Psst." The low hissing sound carried softly across the stables.

"Where's Paxton?" Placing his hat on his head, Owen looked left then right for his brother.

"Psst."

Hearing the low sound again, Owen looked over his left then right shoulder, but couldn't tell where the sound was coming from.

Sean Farraday scratched the jaw of one of the horses Connor had brought over for Adam to shoe at scheduled intervals once the children arrived. "He went looking for Mrs. Neuman. Though I'm still not sure what any of us can do to change this lady's mind."

Morgan stuck his head in the doorway. "Buses are pulling in."

"Time to get this show on the road." Owen turned on his heel and once again heard the hissing noise, only this time a little louder, followed by the soft sound of his name. Looking behind him, spotting a head sticking out from behind the rear barn doors, his Aunt Eileen wiggled a finger at him.

"Aunt Eileen? What the heck are you doing hiding in the stable?"

"I don't want your Uncle Sean to see me."

Owen turned to where his uncle, cousins, and brothers had left to meet the buses. "Slim chance of that. He's halfway down Main Street by now."

"Good." His aunt came out from the shadows. "We have some work to do."

"What are you talking about? We're all ready for the kids."

His aunt shook her head. "The whole town is ready for the kids, that's not what I'm talking about. Do you want to help your girlfriend?"

"Girlfriend?"

"There's no point in fighting it. Gray has spoken."

"Gray?"

"Oh, never mind. Do you want to help get ghostbuster Marla off Connie and Valerie's case or not?"

"Of course I want to help, but what can I do?"

"Then come with me." The way his aunt's smile widened across her face and her chin lifted, he had a feeling whatever was coming next was not going to be good. "Oh." She stopped short. "And we'll need a flashlight."

Flashlight? Whatever he was about to do, he hoped Uncle Sean and Connie weren't going to kill him.

So far Paxton wasn't even a little surprised that this ditzy woman believed in ghosts. She'd explained to him about the positive energy of crystals, which is why she wore a small one on a chain—a 22kt gold chain—and of course the importance of a person knowing their astrological chart. After all, it doesn't pay to make decisions without all the facts. There was something in there about mercury retrograde, but he didn't dare ask her to explain further. Especially since every time he spoke, she sucked in a deep breath and practically shoved her bosom in his face. He didn't mind putting on the charm, but he drew the line at buying what this lady was selling. It was a good thing he loved his sister-in-law and trusted his aunt, otherwise he'd be back there with his brothers and cousins eating and playing with the kids already running around or lining up for front row seats to the cattle drive. "Here we are."

The Parlor House had been this part of Texas' answer to the Chicken Ranch. For decades the brothel was a destination point for military bases, colleges, and restless husbands.

"Ooh, we've been waiting for you." Sissy clapped her hands together and bounced on her feet. "We've never had a real live séance before. I do hope we get to meet Miss Sadie."

"Séance?" Obviously, whatever these women were up to, he hadn't gotten the memo.

"Yes." Sister nodded. "Aunt Eileen offered to conduct the little ghostly effort."

"This will be my first." The shorter of the two sisters beamed.

Sister waved her arm through the foyer. "This is the portrait of Miss Sadie."

"Excellent." Marla closed her eyes and touched the frame.

Paxton looked at the two sisters and wondered why they were buying into all this. Following the ladies, to his surprise, the area he knew as the breakfast bar sat in near darkness. Heavy drapes had been drawn closed. Overhead lights were barely on dim. The furniture had been rearranged to focus on a central round table with a red tablecloth with a massive candle dead center, and his Aunt Eileen with her longtime friends Barbara and Ruth Ann seated waiting. What did these women have up their sleeves?

CHAPTER SIXTEEN

"Sorry I'm late." Connie hurried into the room where everyone was seated. She had no idea what Eileen had up her sleeve, but at least here, maybe Marla Neuman would feel at home.

"Now we can get started." Eileen closed her eyes for a few long moments and leaned over the lit candle, waving her fingers in the same motion someone might use to pull taffy.

With her eyes closed, Eileen Farraday began mumbling to herself before raising her arms and speaking. "Our dearly loved Miss Sadie, we humbly come to call on you."

All Connie asked herself was how could anyone believe in such hokum.

Continuing to wave her hands and keep her eyes closed, Eileen continued to speak in a deep soft spoken tone. "Miss Sadie, we are bringing your town back to life, but we need your guidance."

Sneaking a peek at Mrs. Neuman, Connie could see the woman searching the air in expectation of... what? A voice? An apparition? The woman probably expected the deceased Miss Sadie, the original madame and founder of the town, to stroll into the room and sit down at the table with her.

"If you can hear us, Miss Sadie, let us know."

Everyone sat in total silence. Connie had no idea if this crazy effort would actually work to dissuade Marla Neuman from insisting on her concept of brothel bling, but under the table Connie kept her fingers crossed. Hopefully this didn't end with Marla insisting they needed to redo the Parlor House in brothel bling as well.

"Miss Sadie, if you can hear us, knock twice." How Eileen kept a straight face, Connie had no idea.

Nothing happened and Connie expected Marla to cry foul and storm off any second, forcing Owen to blow the budget while Connie figured out how to create brothel chic, because there was no way in heaven she was using pink fur to decorate. Ready to admit the effort was futile, Connie came within an inch of standing and telling Marla she would start incorporating pink when a rap softly tapped in the distance. Pretty much everyone's eyes opened wide as they listened for more signs. Except for Eileen. The lady could have been a headliner at a carnival. Her eyes still closed, she was playing the part to perfection.

Silence fell and all heads turned to Eileen again. Connie had to give the woman credit. What a performance. Before another word was spoken two clear raps sounded from across the room. Not that Connie believed in ghosts—she didn't—but the hairs on the back of her neck bristled. "Miss Sadie, for the unbelievers in the room, knock once if it's really you."

One strong, loud knock sounded in response and Connie actually jumped in her seat, the hairs on the back of her neck standing straight on edge. Who was doing the knocking? Or could it be what?

Silence settled once again in the large room. Connie didn't understand what was happening. Was this all just a wonderful ruse, or was it time to run for the hills? She looked around the room and everyone was staring intently at the candle that Eileen was once again waving her hand over. Except for Paxton. The expression on his face was more akin to having been asked to eat fried porcupine.

"Miss Sadie. We need your wisdom. Won't you talk to us?" Eileen remained with her eyes closed.

Suddenly, the wall sconces went from dimmed to dark and someone, or two someones, let out a startled gasp. For the life of her, Connie couldn't remember if the lights were on dimmer switches. Of course they had to be. Didn't they? Someone was standing in the shadows controlling the lights. They had to be, except, straining as she tried, she couldn't see a blessed person anywhere in the room. Right about now she didn't know who was more spooked, her or the ghostbuster whose gaze darted about the room at a rapid clip. Connie should have found and dragged Owen to come with her.

"Miss Sadie. There's somebody here who is anxious to talk with you. Won't you come before us?"

A soft breeze blew across the table making the candle flicker. Connie heard her own intake of breath as well as Ruth Ann's beside her. Would anyone notice if she slid out of her seat and crawled out the door?

Any other time or place and the sound of something bumping in the distance would have brought about mild curiosity. Right about now, in the pitch black room, any sound had her ready to jump out of her skin. When another rush of air blew over the table stronger than the one before, a chill traveled through her all the way to her toes. This was crazy. She was letting her imagination get away from her. So what if the inside of an old brothel was drafty? So what if it creaked? Old houses did all of the above. So what if a portrait of a nineteenth century madam floated through the air into the… *floated*?

Not till this very moment in time did Connie understand the meaning of her heart in her throat. She squeezed her eyes tightly shut and then opening one eye came face to face with the portrait of the original Miss Sadie that had been in the foyer and now sat in an empty chair.

"Oh, my." Sissy had gone pale as, well, a ghost.

Connie was pretty sure she didn't look any better. If this was all Eileen Farraday's doing, exactly how did she do it?

"Talk to us, Miss Sadie."

The portrait tilted left than right and Connie did her best to find the strings. There had to be strings. Didn't there?

Eileen let out a dramatic sigh. "Shall we go back to knocking?"

Two more raps on a far wall sounded and Sister's eyes rounded so wide Connie could actually see a rim of white all around the dark irises.

"Very well," Eileen continued. "Are you happy with the

work the Sisters have done with your Parlor?"

Two knocks rapped on the wall and the Sisters visibly blew out sighs of relief.

"Good. Good. And the hotel?"

Another two raps.

"You like the hotel?" This time it was Marla who dared to speak up. Hearing two more raps, Marla's eyes narrowed as she stared at the painting. "I don't believe it."

At that, Eileen groaned loudly, her back stiffened and for the first time she opened her eyes wide as if she'd finally seen a ghost herself. "There's an angry spirit in the room."

Oh, hell. Wasn't it bad enough they had dancing portraits? Connie had to get a grip, but this was just too spooky for her taste.

"Who are you, spirit?"

"Miss Sadie's lost lover." The decidedly male voice had everyone at the table stiffening. Even Ruth Ann tightened her grip on Connie's hand. "Sadie is mine. You can't have her."

Connie swallowed hard as Ruth Ann nearly crushed her fingers.

"Yours?" Eileen almost squeaked. It was the first sign of any emotion the family matriarch had shown. So much so, that Connie looked at the painting again and tried desperately to find wires, anything to prove this was all one giant farce and not a room full of ghosts.

"You can have your town and your tourists, but I keep Sadie."

"But we need her for the hotel," Marla called out. The look in the woman's eyes had gone from curious to desperate.

Where before a chilly breeze had blown by, the second a bit stronger, now another strong wind blew lifting the ends of the tablecloth and sending goose bumps up Connie's arm.

"No," the angry voice hollered as a bright light shone behind Eileen. The light showcasing a face. A man's face. "You need to leave Sadie in peace. Leave the hotel in peace. You need to leave."

Now as white as Sissy and Sister had turned, Marla wasn't so quick to respond. Then, as if gathering her wits and senses again, she squinted at the apparition behind Eileen. Her mouth fell open, her eyes rounded and she turned to Paxton then back to the apparition and once again faced Paxton beside her and shouted, "It's you!"

"Me?" Poor Paxton appeared more confused than concerned. Too bad Connie couldn't say the same thing. She was totally not sure what of all this was Eileen Farraday and what was good reason to high tail it out of there.

"Yes." Marla lifted an arm and jabbed him in the side, then whipped her head back toward the grim voice. "I...I don't understand. The ghost looks exactly like you."

"You leave my descendants alone. Better yet. You just leave."

Now the ghostbuster stiffened in her seat, turned to Paxton and back to the dark space where a well lit Farraday face had stared down at them. The color returning to her face, her shoulders stiffened with indignation. "Well, I never."

Like a strike of lightening, the light under the familiar face came on, and scowling, the voice grew louder. "Go home." When she didn't budge, a chair on the other side of the room lifted into the air and came crashing back down. Once again Connie looked for a shadowed person, any signs of strings, but nothing. Her mouth had gone dry and her palms were sweaty.

The voice boomed again. "I said leave now!"

The flashlight went off, the lights came on, the air from the vents blew surprisingly warm. All set to face a stubborn ghostbuster and gently, or not so gently, suggest that remaining in Sadieville might anger the ghost, at the sound of Marla Neuman's heels clicking loudly halfway down the hall, apparently Connie didn't have to say another word. Looking to Paxton, who seemed to be biting back a smile and offered nothing more than a lazy shrug, Connie glanced at the others, the sisters and Ruth Ann were slowly getting color back in their cheeks, but Connie still hadn't a clue what the heck had just happened, but whatever it was, she sure was happy the Farradays were on her side.

"Oh man, I didn't think that was going to be so much fun." Owen placed the flashlight back in the drawer and turned to one of the foster teens, Kyle. The kid had spotted him and Aunt Eileen walking purposely down the street and asked where they were going if the gun fight was happening on the street any minute.

His aunt had sized the kid up and down and leveling her gaze with his, put her hands on her hips. "You any good at keeping secrets?"

The kid nodded.

"What about pulling pranks?"

The kids smile beamed. "That's easy."

Aunt Eileen bobbed her head. "Got another friend who can keep a secret too? Maybe a little shorter than you?"

"Maybe?" Apparently foster kids weren't as trusting, or maybe the word was gullible. After all, Owen agreed to his aunt's shenanigans without asking any questions. This kid just might have been smarter than Owen.

"Good." Aunt Eileen nodded. "Go get him and meet me behind the Parlor over there. And run. Get this right and there's a twenty in it for each of you."

The kid turned and bolted down the street, reappearing a few minutes later with a little kid at his side. It took his aunt a little while to grab some black clothes from the Mercantile in the right size. Thanking heaven every inch of the way for black jeans and black long sleeve t-shirts turned inside out. By the time his aunt was done with the boys they looked like Halloween skeleton costume without the bones. Even now, he had no idea how on such short notice she had pulled off the perfect costume to hide them in the dark, but she had.

And the boys had done just as she'd told them. The little one had carried the portrait into the room, standing directly behind him to make his outline less obvious. Kyle had managed to turn off the lights, rap on the wall when called for, and blow the fan over a glass of ice water. Of course, he lowered and raised the central air conditioning as well, imitating an angry ghost beautifully. As for Owen's role, his aunt insisted that a live and dead Paxton would successfully freak out the ghostbuster, and of course his aunt had been correct.

"What the heck did you do to Mrs. Neuman?" Valerie came hurrying into Parlor House. "I was just talking with Mr. Neuman, who agreed that your numbers were spot on, the risks were spot on, along with the hotel and the shows rating success, but if his wife wanted pink, then his wife could have pink. I almost cried and then Mrs. Neuman came running out, grabbed her husband by the arm and hauling him to the limo in the parking lot, shouted over her shoulder at me to keep the hotel the way it is and do anything we want with the town."

The only thing blowing up more dust than Mrs. Neuman's limo pulling out of the parking lot at the speed of a Formula 1 racecar were the longhorns making their way to main street for the makeshift cattle drive.

Aunt Eileen sidled up beside Valerie and turned to the two boys at Owen's side. "Here you go, fellows. Twenty a piece as promised, and a bonus for doing the job so well. Now go back with your friends and enjoy your day."

"I repeat," Valerie looked to Owen, "what happened?"

Aunt Eileen shrugged. "She wanted ghosts. So we gave her ghosts."

CHAPTER SEVENTEEN

Still in costume from the last day of the Palooza, most of the Farradays and the Ladies Afternoon Social Club and the sisters sat in rockers on the back porch of the Farraday ranch.

Connie had come from a large family, and she'd always thought they were pretty close, but she doubted they could have pulled off anything like what this clan managed. Not just the roaring success of the Palooza, or the way personalities never seemed to clash within the family businesses, and for sure the way they came together at the last minute to scare off the brothel bling ghostbuster, but here despite an exhausting few days, sharing the love and friendship in the peace and quiet of the evening.

"I think we should do this every year." Eileen took a sip of her drink.

Owen lifted one brow at her. "The séance?"

"Well," Eileen smiled, "I suppose we could put on some kind of show for tourists, but I meant the Palooza. Those kids had a great time."

"That they did." Sean nodded. "A few kids who seemed awfully quiet on day one had come out of their shells by the time they went home today."

"Who knows, maybe we'll have a bunch of good cowhands in a few years." Finn patted his wife's knee and took a sip of his beer.

Joanna smiled up at her husband. "Once this ranching business gets under your skin, it's here to stay."

"Here, here." Sean raised his beer bottle in a toast. "To the ranching life."

Multiple voices chorused the man's sentiments.

Connie almost added *to family*.

"Any word from the sponsors?" Paxton turned to Valerie.

"Nope."

"Uh oh," Meg muttered.

Valerie shook her head. "Not at all. It's been a full forty eight-hours since y'all successfully chased off the ditzy wife. Had there been a problem, weekend or not, I would have heard by now."

"So you don't think we're getting canceled?" Paxton asked.

"Except for Marla's fascination with bling, the sponsors are very happy with the show's ratings. Word on the grapevine before this weekend was that we're in the bag for another season."

"Another season?" several voices echoed.

Valerie shrugged. "Don't sound so shocked. I told all of you that it was a great premise."

"Yeah," Morgan nodded, "but there are only so many buildings in that little town."

"I guess we'll just have to find something else for the Construction Cousins to fix up."

She wasn't sure which of the brothers groaned, but from the look on Paxton and Quinn's faces, maybe everything wasn't all that rosy in the television construction business. Or maybe moving around multiple states was starting to get old for the brothers. Her gaze scanned the people on the porch. This place, and family, definitely grew on a person.

"Too bad Uncle Patrick couldn't stay longer." Adam dropped his booted foot onto his knee. "I barely got to say hello."

"Which reminds me." Eileen pushed to her feet, scurried inside, the porch door slamming shut behind her once on the way in, and seconds later on the way back out. Taking her seat again, she handed her husband an old scrapbook photo album. "I found this old album from when you and your cousins were young."

A wave of sadness crossed Sean Farraday's face before he straightened and plastered on a smile, tapping one of the photos before handing the album over to Paxton beside him. "I think now he'll be back."

Where most of the Texas Farradays nodded or grunted their agreement, the Oklahoma siblings seemed less convinced. Paxton in particular locked gazes with his twin. The two stared for a moment, and then as true mirrored images, nodded and blew out matching sighs. Funny how the two brothers could look so much alike, and yet, Paxton wasn't the one who made her stomach flutter and her heart skip a beat. Looking down at the album again, Paxton whistled. "Holy, moly."

"What?" Sean Farraday looked up at his wide eyed nephew.

"Did Dad used to date Aunt Anne?" Paxton handed the album over to Owen.

Examining the photos, Owen flipped a page. "Wait. Not just date. Engaged." His head snapped up. Now all the Oklahoma Farradays stared at their uncle, mouths slightly agape like landed trout.

Sean Farraday shrugged. "Old news. Water under the bridge a very long time ago."

"Did Mom know?" Morgan accepted the album. "Cause if she didn't that could certainly explain her obsession with staying away from Texas."

"That's not it." The patriarch shook his head. "She knew about it, but by then Anne and Brian were very happily married and already had Ian. And your father was obviously head over boot heels in love with your mom. That wasn't it."

Eileen's mouth drew into a straight line as concern flickered in eyes that studied her husband. Slapping her hands on her knees, she pushed upright. "I say it's time for dessert. Anyone interested, follow me into the kitchen."

Of course, just about every person on the porch caravanned after their aunt into the kitchen. Morgan closed the album and the brothers glanced at each other, Owen was the first to shrug and take a step back. Connie had barely stood from the rocker when Owen came up beside her. "Stay a minute."

She had no idea what he wanted, but she did know one thing: if he'd asked her to lasso the moon, she would have tried.

All evening, Owen had watched how Connie interacted with the members of his family. The woman was truly amazing. She'd taken the whole—as far as he was concerned—seriously weird séance episode in stride.

Waiting until he and Connie were the only two on the porch, he inched closer. "Go for a walk?"

Her head bobbed. At night without a full moon, pitch black easily enveloped the property. Most of the family could walk from house to barn by mere muscle memory. Thankful for an excuse to hold her hand, he extended his arm to help her off the porch into the darkness of the unlit foot path. As if summoned by name, Gray appeared out of nowhere to walk at their side.

"Sweet dog." Connie paused to scratch behind his ears.

From the corner of his eye, Owen spotted his aunt at the kitchen window. No doubt she'd been watching them with the dog. He loved his aunt but she had this nonsensical obsession with Gray's matchmaking skills. The dog was simply, well, a dog. And yet, here he was walking with Connie and thinking for the first time in his life that he never wanted his time with her to end.

His brothers and he had been discussing the next steps of the business, both the show and the other projects. And their mother. At least since his father left Oklahoma, she'd stopped blowing up his phone. Hopefully his father would be able to talk some sense into her or else she was going to miss Neil and Nora's wedding because this time the bride was from Tuckers Bluff, but his mother and her relationship with Texas was fodder for another day.

Connie tilted her face upward. "No matter how many nights I look up at the sky in this part of the state, the beauty never ceases to amaze me. So many lights."

"It is beautiful. I have to admit, living out here is really growing on me."

Her face tilted up to the sky. "I can see why."

"We, uh, are discussing taking on more jobs in this neck of the woods and fewer in our home state."

"Really?" Her expression remained a blank slate telling him nothing of how she felt.

He nodded. "Really. We've also, well, I've also wondered if you like these stars enough to work on more projects here."

"That would have little to do with how I feel about the West Texas skies and more to do with where Harriet assigns me."

"Yeah, well." His hand hooked around that back of his neck. "About that."

Her gaze remained focused on him.

"You told me once you're grown up dream was to work for yourself."

She nodded.

"What if you were to work with us?"

"I already do that."

"I don't mean for Harriet. I mean for you."

Her eyes narrowed, her brows buckled, and she paused to consider his words.

"The Farraday brothers would only use your firm to design for our clients. Clients who will more and more be right here in Texas."

"Wait." Her eyes grew wide and her mouth fell slightly open. "You want me to start my own firm and work exclusively for you?"

"Oh, no. You can work for whoever you like, we would be the ones to exclusively use you. This way you would always be assured a reasonable living."

"Why are you doing this?" Dark brown eyes stared intently into his eyes.

He suspected saying *because I love you* wasn't the right response. "Because you're good."

"Thank you, but so is Harriet. Why me? Why not Tammy?"

"I love Tammy—"

Connie's eyes rounded and he immediately back-pedaled.

"As a friend. I love her as a friend. But everyone agrees you're better than Tammy, and Harriet has plenty of work besides us to keep her office busy."

"That she does." Connie stared up at the sky again. "I'd have to think about this. It's a big step giving up a full time paying job to chase a dream."

"Dreams are always worth chasing." He stepped into her space and wrapped his arms around her waist, then leaned in. The moment his lips met hers, any thoughts he'd pondered about how he felt for Connie were confirmed. Beyond the shadow of any doubt, she was the woman for him. Wishing he could kiss her like this under the stars for now and for always, the practical side of him knew better. Sharing one last peck on those soft pliable lips, he took a step back. "I don't know if this makes any difference, or if it will chase you away, but I'm falling head over boot heels in love with you."

She blinked. "Is that why you're offering me the chance at my dream of my own business?"

He ran the pad of this thumb down her cheek and shook his head. "Not a chance. I'm a numbers man through and through and don't give false praise. I'm offering you our business because you're really good at what you do. And maybe," he tipped his head back with a smile, "it might have helped that you roll really well with the punches. Not everyone can keep up with Aunt Eileen, stand up to the Marla Neuman's of the world, or put up with my spending control. Whether you say yes or no to the offer, my feelings for you won't change."

A bright smile took over her face and lit her eyes. "Good thing then, because I feel the same way." She threw her arms around his neck. "I'll follow you wherever you go."

"I was hoping you'd say that."

Gray sat on his haunches and let out a loud quick bark. Pulling her back into his arms for another kiss, the thought crossed his mind that maybe, just maybe, his aunt and this dog knew something the rest of them didn't.

EPILOGUE

"I've never been so excited about a project coming together in my whole life." Connie stood in the middle of the street staring at the bright pink ribbon stretched from post to post in front of the Hotel Grande.

"The name suits the place." Paxton and the other Farradays had little to do with the naming of the hotel. In the end, the city council received an offer for the hotel that they simply could not refuse. Though they had yet to see or meet a representative of the new company in person, the management team sent to finalize details seemed to fully understand the little things that separated an ordinary luxury hotel from a five star deluxe luxury hotel. Even Paxton wouldn't mind a quiet weekend in one of the rooms. The introductory rates were in place until the hotel and spa were fully ready for patrons, making a short stay more practical for a working man. Still, the place glistened with extravagant yet simple décor. Connie had nailed it every step of the way. As a matter of fact, Pax was convinced it was the genius of his brother's design and Connie's packaging that made the sale so easy. The city council was happy, the network was happy, the sponsors were happy. All in all, a happy day all around.

"Come on," Owen squeezed Connie's hand and tugged her forward, "time to cut the ribbon."

"Not me." She took a step back. "I'm just the interior designer."

Owen leaned into her and gently kissed her temple. "Didn't I tell you?"

Lifting her gaze to meet his, her eyes narrowed. "Tell

me what?"

Pax took a step back and shook his head. When would his brother learn that springing things last minute on the women in your life was never a good idea.

"He'll learn." Aunt Eileen elbowed her nephew and smiled.

"Learn what?" His aunt had many a talent, but he refused to believe reading minds was one of them.

She chuckled. "Doesn't pay to keep secrets from your partner, especially ones that involve public presentations."

Okay, Pax blew out a sigh, maybe the woman could read minds, just a little. But none of that took away from the murmurs taking place between his twin and his new love. Though if Pax was any judge of the stars in those two's eyes, this was going to be another lifelong love like his brothers and cousins had found.

Another few moments and Owen kissed his girl ever so slightly, nodded at her, and Pax knew when she nodded back that Connie had just agreed to help cut the ribbon. All the brothers had agreed that Neil had created a brilliant plan to convert the dilapidated old structure into the twenty first century, but it was Connie's understanding of the project and eye for detail that brought Neil's designs to life. It was only reasonable for her to be involved in the ribbon cutting, it just wasn't so smart of his brother to wait for the last minute to tell her.

"They do make a cute couple." Aunt Eileen stood to one side watching as Neil and Connie and the Tuckers Bluff mayor held the massive scissors and snipped at the ribbon.

As soon as the ribbon fell to the ground, Connie spun around and threw her arms around Owen's neck. The two exchanged a short but sweet peck on the lips before walking into the building holding hands. The sight gave Pax a thump in his chest. For all of his life he and Owen had been a team of two. Pax loved and got along with all his brothers, but Owen was different, special, they were almost like the same person in so many ways. They would always share a special bond that none of the other brothers did, but Pax knew that even so, things would never be quite the same. Connie would be the bigger part of Owen's life. And Pax was okay with that, but it still was going to take a little getting used to.

"Shall we?" Aunt Eileen extended her elbow. "Toni made her mini Boston cream tarts."

"Oh, that woman can bake." Readjusting his aunt's arm for her hand to link with his forearm, he took a step forward. The grand opening committee had confiscated the empty building next door that would eventually be the spa. In the center a large wooden dance floor had been set up with café tables all around. To one side a band was playing soft but uplifting tunes while people filled their plates with the food that the pub and café and Molly had provided. A sampling of the area's best.

"Someone's going to have to get this party started." Aunt Eileen looked Pax in the eyes. "Care to take a turn on the floor?"

"Me?" He almost laughed out loud. "I guess you haven't heard. I have two left feet. I've been banned at weddings from dancing in a crowd."

His aunt burst out laughing. "Oh, you can't be that bad."

"Oh, I can. Trust me." He pointed to Owen. "He inherited the *twinkle toes* gene."

At that moment, Owen raised Connie's hand in his, tipped his head at the bandleader, and with the first beat of the fast paced rhythm, the two were cutting the proverbial rug.

"Oh, my." Aunt Eileen's jaw dropped open. "You weren't kidding."

"Nope."

His aunt's gaze scanned the room. When her eyes landed on Uncle Sean, her smile widened and any idiot could feel the love arcing across the room. Another moment and his uncle had crossed the room and escorted his wife onto the dance floor. Apparently Uncle Sean and Owen had inherited the dancing gene from the same ancestor. Maybe his aunt could teach him a step or two. Most women he knew all seemed to love to dance. Even now, his brother and uncle were the only two couples on the floor, all the rest were the ladies bopping around and laughing as if they were young teens again.

A slower song came on and his brother twirled Connie into the fold of his arms, and just like the movie, dipped her. Pax actually heard the combined gasps of delight from several women standing around him. When Owen lifted her upright and kissed her more deeply than he'd ever seen his brother do in public, the maneuver cemented Pax's suspicion that another of his brothers had fallen head over boot heel forever in love. The only thought that rummaged about in his foot loose and fancy free bachelor mind was: *wouldn't it be nice.*

Excerpt from
Just One Date

"**O**ur grandfather, a man richer than Bezos, offered to pay for the wedding, and the future Mrs. Andrew Mason told him no?" Chase James Baron, head of Baron Enterprises and confirmed bachelor, tipped his brandy snifter at his sister Eve. "The more I learn about Nancy, the more I like her."

As far as their grandfather, a former Marine turned politician, was currently concerned, each of his grandchildren should have six children – just as he and his wife of sixty years had done. Andrew's mother, Amanda Baron Mason, was the youngest and closest in age to Chase's father, Bradley Baron. Bradley had garnered his father's approval by marrying young, and well, although he only had five children, instead of the expected six. Unfortunately for Bradley, divorcing Chase's mother and working his way through three more wives had not gone over nearly as well with the proud former governor. Even if the unions had added two more grandchildren to the fold.

Now their grandfather was clearly tiring of waiting for his grandchildren to continue the tradition of having a large family. So far, much to former Governor James Earnest Baron's chagrin, every last one of his progeny was woefully behind the curve in finding a spouse and increasing the troops – his loving reference to his family. Except for Andrew, who had been caught and reeled in by his new bride-to-be.

Andrew and Nancy's nuptials had brought Chase to Galveston in preparation of the first, long-awaited, wedding of his generation. He and his siblings, Craig, Mitch and Eve were waiting for their brother Kyle onboard his yacht—a favorite family gathering spot—to leave for a quiet sail along the Gulf coast before the upcoming festivities, and ensuing chaos began.

"You're going to love Nancy," his sister Eve said with a smile. "Smart and sassy. Perfect for Andrew. Even though the Governor grumbles about her stubbornness—often—I think he really likes her."

"If it means finally having a great-grandchild, I think he'd let Lucrezia Borgia into the fold." Chase would have laughed at his own joke if he didn't think it held a grain of truth. "At least Andrew and Nancy will take the pressure off the rest of us grandchildren to breed."

Eve almost snorted her brandy. "What planet are you living on? If anything it's made the Governor more determined to increase the family troops. Oh, wait. That's right. You hide out in your Dallas man cave. Sleep, eat, and breathe Baron Enterprises. I must say, moving the operations to the downtown high rise, including a penthouse apartment, made for an affordable commute. You never even have to leave the building. Ever."

"Now you sound like the old man." Ten years ago when Chase had first come up with the mixed-use plans for the new headquarters, his grandfather had been delighted with the idea. Chase and his cousin Devlin, founder of one of the largest commercial real estate firms in the country, had worked out every detail before presenting it to their grandfather. That had been long before the patriarch had become obsessed with seeing his grandchildren procreate.

"*Never gonna meet a good woman if you live behind that desk. Balance, boy. Balance,*" Chase mimicked his grandfather.

"*You can take the man out of the military, but you can't take the military out of the man. Push, push, push.*" Eve tipped her head back and blew out a sigh. "Did you hear what he did to Craig?"

"At Mitch's fund-raiser last month?"

Eve nodded. "Craig made the mistake of telling the Governor that he was going stag to our dear brother the senator's event."

"Craig runs a major production company. Surely an up-and-coming actress would have been more than happy to have her photos splattered across every media outlet under the sun at a ten-thousand-dollar-a-plate dinner for the senate's golden boy."

"I don't think any of us realized the Governor has upped the ante. If we can't find our own dates, he'll find someone for us."

"And that is exactly why I am bringing my own date." Chase pushed to his feet and crossed the lounge of his brother's yacht to refill his drink. One of the stuffiest families on the social registry, the Van Kleins had married off all their children but one. And from his limited interactions with Gwyneth, her spinsterhood was for good reason. "I can't help but wonder, what was the Governor thinking, sticking Craig all night with Gwyneth Van Klein?"

Eve raised a single brow at her eldest brother, then shook her head. "The usual. Good stock. Wide hips. I swear, in this day and age, the old man still thinks of women as brood mares. He probably has Gwyneth's dental records."

"I'd be more worried that he probably has yours." Kyle, the missing sibling, came through the doorway. "Sorry I'm late. My meeting ran long. I see you've already helped yourself to refreshments."

"We skipped the lemonade and went straight for the hard stuff." Eve smiled up at him.

"My Napoleon brandy." Kyle laughed. "Rough week?"

"The Governor gave me a lecture on my biological clock yesterday. And the day before—"

"And this morning," Kyle added, his eyes filled with sympathy. "Sorry, sis."

"I'm used to it. It's not like I don't want to meet a nice guy, but it's not easy when your last name is Baron."

Unfortunately, Chase knew exactly what she meant. Having a family fortune prominently reported for all to see, the Baron name was a golden ticket for swindlers and fortune hunters. He'd been there, done that, even bought the wardrobe. Which is why he'd decided, before ever setting foot near Galveston for his cousin's wedding, to preempt the former Governor's unwanted efforts to find his offspring suitable mates. Chase might not run a major film production company, but he'd seen *Pretty Woman*. While he wasn't stupid enough to hire a hooker to appease his grandfather's matchmaking attempts, Chase wasn't beyond hiring a good actress to redirect their grandfather's attention elsewhere.

The plan had merit. Strictly business. No emotions. No gold diggers. And best of all, no complications.

"You're getting paid to spend the next seven days with a man?" C. J. Lawson's head was ready to explode from her sister's latest crazy plan.

"Yes and no." Bev shrugged.

C.J. glared at her younger sister the same way she'd stare down a raw recruit and then drew upon years of military discipline not to scream in Bev's face. "You do realize those answers do not go together."

"Yes, for five thousand dollars now and five thousand at the end of the week, I'm being paid to spend one week with Chase Baron but no not '*with*' with him."

"Do you know where you're staying?"

"Galveston."

C.J. refrained from rolling her eyes at her Pollyanna-like sister. "In a hotel?"

Nibbling on her lower lip, Bev hesitated a few minutes. "Maybe. He might have mentioned a boat."

"Okay." Who would have thought dealing with boots fresh off the bus would be easier than shaking some sense into her starry-eyed sister? "Maybe in a hotel, or a boat, but definitely in separate rooms?"

"Oh." Bev stopped tossing clothes into her suitcase. "I didn't ask."

Oh, brother. Never before had C.J. wished so hard that

Bev had gotten a few less beauty genes and just a teensy-weensy bit more of the brains in the family. At five foot five and 110 pounds, with a twenty-four inch waist, and blue eyes the shade of an azure crayon, Bev conjured images of Marilyn Monroe, Judy Holiday, and a long list of talented women who got more from sex appeal than smarts. "How could you not ask about sleeping arrangements?"

"Because, for ten thousand dollars, I don't really care if he puts me on the roof."

"Or in his bed?"

Sweater in hand, Bev froze and looked up at her sister. "That wasn't part of the negotiations."

All set to ask "What negotiations?" since her sister didn't seem to have any answers other than a 10K salary in a one-week time frame, and something about fooling an old man, C.J.'s mind suddenly registered that Bev held a sweater. "Why are you packing cold-weather clothes for Galveston?"

"Oh, well, that's what I was getting around to explaining."

That pixie twinkle in Bev's eye was never a good sign. As a kid it could have meant anything from teaching the unwilling cat how to swim, to homemade hair dye. Neither of which had produced stellar results. "Then explain. Again."

"Okay." Bev flipped her long blonde hair behind her shoulder and sucked in a deep breath. "Chase's cousin is getting married in eight days. It's a big family wedding. All the siblings and cousins and aunts and uncles will be there. Even his mom, who is practically a hermit somewhere in Europe, is crossing the pond for her favorite nephew's wedding."

C.J. bobbed her head, encouraging her sister to get to whatever part of this plan she hadn't already heard.

"So Chase has this grandfather."

"Yes," C.J. quipped a bit impatiently. "You've mentioned that before. He wants to see all his grandchildren married. I got that part."

"Well, the Governor—"

"Governor?"

"That's the grandfather. Former governor of Texas, though I think it was a lot of years ago, and before that he was a Marine."

"*Is*," C.J. said without thinking.

"Oh, yeah." Bev sighed and echoed with her sister, "*Once a Marine, always a Marine.*"

"Right." C.J. nodded again, sorry she'd derailed her sister's story.

"To avoid the grandfather harassing and annoying and prodding and matchmaking and creating family drama at his cousin's wedding, I've been hired to be his date. Like *Pretty Woman.*"

"You do remember she was a hooker?"

"Julia Roberts?"

Lord, C.J. loved her sister. Really she did. But the girl had tested C.J.'s patience from the day their parents had brought Bev home from the hospital. "Vivian—the character in the movie—Vivian was a hooker."

"Oh, yeah. Whatever. He offered me 10K to be his date." Bev stopped and, biting on her lower lip again, raised her gaze to the ceiling in thought. "Maybe it was *girlfriend.*" Smiling, she bobbed her head. "That was it. His girlfriend for a week."

"*Girlfriend.*" C.J. could hear the whine in her voice. She hated people who whined. "And you didn't ask about sleeping arrangements?" Why couldn't Bev be something normal, like a manicurist or receptionist? Why an actress? "Never mind. Can we get back to the clothes?"

"Oh. Right." Bev perked up. "This morning I got a call from my friend Gloria. You remember Gloria?"

C.J. nodded. She had no clue who the heck Gloria was, but C.J. had no intention of letting this conversation go down another rabbit hole.

"Gloria got a small part in John Cipro's new movie. It's a minor character, but they need a lot of extras because they're filming out in the middle of nowhere, and she got me on the list of extras! If they like me, I might even get to say something." Bev practically jumped in place with glee.

"At least that's a legitimate gig. When does filming start?"

"Monday."

"This Monday?" Now C.J. was really confused.

"Yes. In Canada, where it's cold."

At least that explained the sweater. "So, why are we having this conversation, if you're not taking the job in Galveston?"

"Because you are."

MEET CHRIS

Author of dozens of contemporary novels, including the award winning Aloha Series, Chris Keniston lives in suburban Dallas with her husband, two human children, and two canine children. Though she loves her puppies equally, she admits being especially attached to her German Shepherd rescue. After all, even dogs deserve a happily ever after.

More on Chris and her books can be found at www.chris keniston.com.

Follow Chris on facebook at ChrisKenistonAuthor or on twitter @ckenistonauthor.

Join Chris' newsletter! Enjoy inside peeks and photographs from Chris' world and stories. Some times she'll thank her subscribers with a free copy of a new 99 cent flirt.

Please, if you enjoyed reading Owen, consider helping other readers find the Farraday Country Series by taking a moment to leave a review. Reviews are a blessing to authors and readers alike. Even just a few words will do! Thank you.

www.ingramcontent.com/pod-product-compliance
Lightning Source LLC
Chambersburg PA
CBHW031418200726
48285CB00017BA/2440